M000073715

No Police
Like Holmes

Introducing Sebastian McCabe

Second Edition

Dan Andriacco

Paperback ISBN 978-1-78092-847-0
ePub ISBN 978-1-78092-848-7
PDFISBN 978-1-78092-849-4

Published in the UK by MX Publishing
335 Princess Park Manor, Royal Drive,
London, N11 3GX
www.mxpublishing.com
Cover design by www.staunch.com

This book is fondly dedicated to

PAUL D. HERBERT, B.S.I.

and members of the Tankerville Club,
past and present —
they are nothing like the Sherlockians in this book!

CONTENTS

Chapter One
Murder, She Said

Lynda Teal, my former lady love, had lied to me.

Looking back now, I realize that wasn't the only possible explanation for why she had driven away from her apartment instead of toward it after telling me she was going home to change her clothes. But it was the only one that occurred to me at the time.

She was up to something and she was dealing me out. Was it a line on the crime we'd been investigating—or some new romantic entanglement? I had to know.

Her bright yellow Mustang was just at the edge of campus, stopped at the traffic light—a notoriously long light. I still had a chance, just a chance, of catching up. I pulled my Schwinn out of the rack behind Muckerheide Center, mounted it, and shoved off, pedaling furiously.

Unseasonably warm wind for March pushed across my face. It was six-twenty on a fine near-spring afternoon, clear and fresh. Birds should have been chirping.

I felt like hell.

Lynda had never lied to me before, so far as I knew. She'd yelled at me, sure, and called me unpleasant names on numerous occasions. But she'd never lied to me when we were a couple. The realization that things were different between us now, and probably always would be, cut into my gut like a butcher knife. I pedaled harder.

I weaved in front of an elderly woman hunched over the wheel of a silver-gray Buick Lucerne. She had her windows up and her air conditioning on, rushing the season by at least a couple of months, so I don't know what she had to say to me, but she was vigorous about it.

By the time the light changed I'd managed to get behind Lynda. Being on two wheels instead of four, I was able with effort to weave myself into what I judged to be her blind spot.

We snaked through downtown Erin, past the Gamble Bank & Trust Co., the Masonic Hall, the Beans & Books coffee house and bookstore (right across the street from Starbucks), the Sussex County Court House, Garrison's Antiques, Daniel's Apothecary, and the offices of the *Erin Observer & News-Ledger*, where Lynda works as news editor. Just as I was beginning to wonder how much longer I could keep up the pace, Lynda turned into the garage of the Winfield Hotel several blocks ahead of me.

Erin also has another quality hotel, the Harridan, and a few chain motels, but the Winfield is the oldest hostelry in this college town, the most elegant, and the closest to campus. Most of the out-of-town participants in the "Investigating Arthur Conan Doyle and Sherlock Holmes" colloquium were staying there.

The lobby had flocked wallpaper, red carpeting, and two banks of three elevators each, with walnut doors. The tan of Lynda's skirt was just disappearing into the farthest elevator when I entered the lobby. The old-fashioned needle above the elevator door slowly swung in a half-moon arc to the number nine as I watched. When the middle elevator opened in front of me and a family with three kids spewed out, I got in and pushed the same number.

My stomach was in Ulcer City on the way up. Here my ex-girlfriend was meeting somebody in a hotel room and it didn't take a sleuth in a deerstalker cap to figure out who and why. That hurt me like I hadn't been hurt since Wendy Kotzwinkle threw me over for a football player in the eleventh grade. (The football player later became a used car salesman, and not a very good one.)

I guess I wasn't over Lynda after all. Who had I been trying to kid?

When the elevator doors opened on the ninth floor, I found myself in an alcove. Feeling like some sleazy private eye—much sleazier than Max Cutter, the hero of the detective novels I write in my all-too-abundant spare time— I peaked around the corner into the main corridor.

Nothing to the right.

I turned my head the other way for a second, then quickly jerked it back before Lynda could see me. She was in the hallway, standing in front of a door, fingering one of the those rectangular pieces of plastic that passes for a hotel key these days.

I risked another look and she was gone, having no doubt disappeared into the room.

Now what the hell should I do?

For some time I essentially did nothing, just stood there waiting for a brainstorm. I didn't get one. Just as I finally started walking tentatively down the hallway toward where I had last seen Lynda, she re-emerged, coming out of the room back first. When she turned around I was right in front of her. Her face was pale, her eyes wild.

"Jeff!" She threw her arms around me. Her body was trembling. Instinctively, I held her tightly. The proximity was not unpleasant.

"What's wrong?" I said finally. "What is it, Lynda?"

"It's murder," she said. "That's what."

Chapter Two
You Call This a Party?

Before the mayhem was all over I was accused of murder and Lynda got conked on the head. But the whole business started innocently enough at a party less than twenty-four hours before she found the body.

Everywhere I looked that night, people were wearing deerstalker caps. Not everybody, mind you, but enough to give the idea that this was no ordinary cocktail party. Which it sure wasn't. From where I stood in my sister's hallway, nursing a caffeine-free Diet Coke, I was bombarded with snatches of strange conversation from the living room on one side and the dining room on the other.

"Of course Sherlock Holmes was illiterate. Why else would he have Watson read everything to him?"

"I'm so tired of Holmes vs. Jack the Ripper stories."

"In fact, Holmes is *still* alive."

This last was proclaimed by one of the deerstalkered gents, a tall, lean specimen in his early forties with a sharp nose. He was holding forth to the living room contingent, a group of half a dozen or so, a few of whom seemed to be actually listening. I stepped into the room for a better look and saw that, sure enough, he was wearing a button that said SHERLOCK HOLMES LIVES!

I didn't hang around for the rest of the lecture. I turned, intending to check out the action in the dining room. At least there was food there. The movement brought me practically nose to nose with the kind of woman you don't often see outside of Greek and Roman statuary: oval face, creamy complexion, wide brown eyes, raven hair spilling over bare shoulders. The simplicity of her black dress was counterbalanced by enough silver at her throat, wrists and ears to keep a crew of Navajo silversmiths in business for a good while.

"But no funny hat," I said.

"Pardon?" The look she gave me was puzzled, but by no means unfriendly.

"Oh, sorry, just thinking out loud," I said. Jeff Cody, Mr. Small Talk, that's me. I didn't even know where to take it from there, that's how out of practice I was at schmoozing with beautiful strangers. This one was in her early thirties, just the age when women get really interesting. She was also tall and nicely built, meaning she knew how to eat but also when to stop.

She smiled at me and said, "Interesting collection of individuals we have here." Was it just my imagination or was she including me in that collection? It wasn't impossible. I'm six-one, reasonably presentable if you like red-headed men, and always careful to dress only slightly out of style as befits my academic environment.

"Interesting is one word for it," I conceded. "No offense, but I've never really understood this whole Sherlockian thing. I mean, I guess the Holmes stories are readable enough, but I don't get the obsession over them. I'm more into hard-boiled private eyes, myself."

She chuckled, a pleasant sound. "Then what are you doing here?"

For a guy who was thirty-six years old and unattached by virtue of being recently thrown over by a woman I was in love with, it marginally beat being alone on a Friday night. But I didn't get into that.

"I'm Professor McCabe's brother-in-law," I confessed, "and also the public relations director at St. Benignus College. This Sherlock Holmes colloquium he's putting on tomorrow is a fairly big deal for us. And the presentation to the school of the Woollcott Chalmers Collection of Sherlockiana is a *really* big deal."

She smiled at my babbling. "That I know all about."

"Part of my job will be to promote it with social media and mass media. And then later I have to do write-ups for the alumni magazine, the annual report, the fund-raising newsletter . . . it's endless. So I'm here to soak up information. Tomorrow I'll be taking notes and tweeting."

I patted the reporter's notebook salted away in my left breast pocket. "Are you one of the speakers?"

Most of the guests at this soirée were, but she shook her head. "I'm afraid I don't have much in common with Sherlock Holmes except that we both play the violin."

Better and better, I thought. "Can I get you a drink?"

"A light beer would be nice."

That shows how wrong you can be about a person. I had pegged her for a white-wine woman.

The drinks were in the bathroom at the other end of the long hall. Sebastian McCabe, husband to my sister, Kate, has a beer tap in his study. But when he throws a party, he fills up the claw-footed first-floor bathtub with ice and lets his guests serve themselves. I fished through the icy water and pulled up . . . Guinness, Kentucky Bourbon Barrel Ale, Edmund Fitzgerald Porter, Rivertown Dunkel. Not exactly light beers. Finally I found a bottle of Samuel Adams Light for—whom? I hadn't even asked her name. I really *was* rusty after four years out of general circulation. For myself, I pulled out another caffeine-free Diet Coke. I know all the studies say that moderate intake of alcohol is actually healthful, but moderation has never been my forte. Besides, I have a history of saying things I shouldn't after just a couple of beers. So I only partake in cases of extreme need or high celebration.

With a bottle in one hand and a can in the other, I was just turning to leave the bathroom when a bright light exploded in my face. For a second all I could see were white spots in front of me. I blinked furiously and the spots made way for a smiling Japanese man with a camera in his hand. My first thought was something like, "Who invited the press to this party?" Then I remembered all the Japanese mystery enthusiasts I'd once seen at a meeting of the Mystery Writers of America in New York. This one was probably a member of the Bartitsu Society, the incredibly huge Sherlock Holmes group in Japan.

No ugly American I, I bowed in his direction and said, "Ohio," which I believe means hello or good morning or something like that. It's the one bit of Japanese I can always remember because it's the state I've lived in since I first came to St. Benignus College from Virginia as a student a couple of decades ago.

But the man with the camera regarded me in obvious puzzlement. "What about Ohio?"

As soon as he opened his mouth, I knew my picture belonged in the dictionary next to the word "fool," with the appropriate synonyms: numbskull, buffoon, knucklehead. The guy didn't have a trace of an accent. He wasn't Japanese at all—he was an American. His parents or grandparents or honorable ancestors even further back must have come from the Land of the Rising Sun, but not him.

"Uh, it's a nice state," I answered lamely. "Where are you from?"

"Philadelphia."

Light dawned. "You must be Bob Nakamora."

He acknowledged as much and I introduced myself. Nakamora was to give a talk on Sunday morning about "Holmes on the Radio." Appropriately, I'd scheduled him for an interview with the campus radio station. I filled him in on the time and where I'd pick him up.

"We'll have to talk about Philadelphia some time," I said. "I write mystery novels about a private detective named Max Cutter who lives there." I've actually only been to Philadelphia a couple of times, but I decided long ago that Erin, Ohio, population 29,098 (although seemingly double that on St. Patrick's Day), was no place for a murder mystery. Too bad I was wrong.

"Oh, sure," Nakamora replied. "I've read a couple of those books."

Unfortunately, that's not possible. None of my five Max Cutter yarns has been published. But I had the feeling that if I didn't leave right away the polite Mr. Nakamora would start telling me how much he liked my work, which is always depressing. I held up the Samuel Adams Light in my hand. "Somebody's waiting for this. Catch you later."

But when I got back to where I'd been a few minutes before, the beautiful woman in black was gone.

Why was I so surprised? Max Cutter would have figured out right away that if she weren't one of the symposium speakers herself then she must have been brought here by one of them. She could have even been married to him. I'd been so dazzled by all that silver that I hadn't checked to see if her jewelry included a ring on the fourth finger of her left hand. But I was betting it did.

I looked around for her anyway. I had her beer. So I wandered into the kitchen for a while, heard a woman in a deerstalker cap say, "Watson must have been good at something; he was married three times!" and wandered back out. In the dining room I waved at my sister, Kate, fair and red-haired like me, who was slicing a knife through a cheese ball. Before I could say a word of greeting, somebody I recognized tried to squeeze past me in the doorway. You would have recognized him, too, even though he looked bigger and tougher on television and on the dust jackets of his books.

"Al Kane," I blurted out.

He nodded wearily, as if tired of a quarter-century in the public eye.

"I'm Jeff Cody. We talked on the phone."

"Right. Good to meet you."

He let his teeth show a smile through the familiar bandit's mustache as he shook my hand. In his mid-fifties, Al Kane wasn't the man he once was—and maybe in reality he never had been. He was only about five-seven or -eight and his rust-colored hair was tinged with gray. His wire-rimmed glasses—which he didn't wear on TV or his book jackets—made him look like an accountant moonlighting as a shoe store clerk, not the author of a dozen blood-and-babes novels. But then, he hadn't come out with a new Red Maddox mystery in five years or more. Too bad. Red had been one of my heroes ever since I was a kid reading with a flashlight under the covers in bed. But all of Kane's energies these days seemed to be devoted to appearances on commercials and talk shows as the pistol-packing spokesman for the National Pistol Association.

I'd called Kane about a week before to set up a telephone interview with Maggie Barton of the *Erin Observer & News-Ledger*, our local outpost of the Grier Media Corp. empire. It had worked out great from my point of view. The resulting story about the symposium was picked up by the Associated Press and used by a lot of other papers. The "Red Maddox meets Sherlock Holmes" angle had gone over big.

"Frankly, I don't understand why you agreed to talk to these Sherlock Holmes fanatics," I told Kane in a low voice as I grabbed an hors d'oeuvre off the dining room table. "The science of deduction doesn't exactly figure in the adventures of Red Maddox."

He shrugged. "Mac asked me to do it."

Sebastian McCabe, the Lorenzo Smythe Professor of English Literature and head of the popular culture program at St. Benignus College, has more friends than I have rejections from publishers. Apparently their ranks include just about the entire membership of the Mystery Writers of America as well as something like 4,374 people on Facebook. You probably know that Mac himself is the author of the popular Damon Devlin mystery series, Devlin being a magician who solves murders on the side. When I tell you that my brother-in-law was once a professional conjuror before he settled down to get a college degree as a non-traditional student, you don't need to be Sigmund Freud to see this as wish fulfillment. I don't think much of these tales, and I don't believe for a minute that Devlin or any other amateur could out-sleuth my Max Cutter in real life. But they sell.

"I've read all your books, including *The Baker Street Caper*," I said to Kane, "and these Sherlockians are going to eat you alive for that one."

Kane took a drink of what appeared to be bourbon, then set down his glass on the dining room table. "That story satirizes the Baker Street Irregular types, not Holmes himself. I respect Holmes as the protagonist of the modern-day private eye of fiction. What I don't like is the game some people play, pretending that Holmes is real and Conan Doyle was nothing more than a literary agent."

"But of course Holmes is real!"

That didn't come from me, you may be sure. The fellow with the Basil Rathbone nose, the one I'd seen in the living room, had butted into the conversation. He introduced himself as Dr. Noah Queensbury, Official Secretary of the Anglo-Indian Club. That's the Holmes group in Cincinnati, about forty miles downriver from Erin, to which Mac and many of the other colloquium participants belonged.Apparently the group took its name from a club mentioned in one of the Sherlock Holmes stories.

"Perhaps you missed my monograph on 'Ten Proofs for the Existence of Sherlock Holmes,'" Queensbury said.

Kane gave me a "What the hell?" look.

"Proof number one." Queensbury held up a finger. "There used to be a Metropolitan Line train on the London underground called *The Sherlock Holmes*. The British do not name trains after fictional characters."

I abandoned my unfinished Diet Coke and opened the Samuel Adams Light. This was not to be endured without fortification. My sister, still hovering over the cheese ball, gave me a weak smile as I swallowed the brew.

"Proof number two," Queensbury droned on. "In 1988, I wrote a letter to Mr. Holmes at 221B Baker Street, London. It was answered by a secretary. Fictional characters do not have secretaries. Proof number three—"

"Wait a minute," I interrupted. "Sherlock Holmes has to be a fictional character. It says so on Wikipedia." I just assumed that, having never looked it up.

Queensbury snorted. "That almost proves my case. Everyone knows Wikipedia is unreliable."

"You're impossible," Kane growled.

"Proof number three—" Queensbury persisted, unruffled.

I'd intended to press Kane on the state of detective fiction for an article in the alumni magazine, but that obviously would have to wait. I had to get out of there before I started screaming. I edged past Queensbury, who didn't seem to notice, and into the now-crowded hallway.

For a minute I felt trapped there amid the dozen or so lunatics gibbering about Sherlock Holmes. Then I spotted Mac on the other side of the hall, sitting by the unlit fire in his thirty-foot living room.

"Ah, Jefferson," he said as I approached. "Driven you to drink, have we?"

He thought he was joking. I know that because he laughed, his bearded chins wobbling above a polka-dot bow tie. With his whale-like body settled in a wingback chair, he looked innocent enough. There was no indication, for example, of his predilection for marching down the college quadrangle clad in a kilt and playing the bagpipes on the first day of every spring semester. There was nothing to tell you that he enjoyed writing a blog critiquing the faulty grammar in official communications around campus, delighting the undergrads and putting half the faculty and administration in an uproar. And there wasn't the slightest hint that he fancied himself a Great Detective lacking only a case. He's my best friend, and the biggest thorn in my side. When we'd first met as college students at St. Benignus he was already something of an *enfant terrible*. Now, pushing forty (three years older than me), he's no longer an *enfant*, but still *terrible*.

"Come and meet Woollcott," he said, waving me into a nearby couch.

Woollcott Chalmers, sitting at the end of the couch closest to Mac, looked to be in his mid- to late-seventies, if the whiteness of his hair and thin mustache weren't deceiving. His eyes, enlarged by lenses in his black-framed glasses, were blue and penetrating. He was impeccably dressed in a black suit and red foulard tie. He held a cane loosely between his legs. I knew from Mac that he'd inherited a few million dollars, increased it about ten-fold during a career of investing money for himself and others, and had never been shy about spending goodly quantities of it on pet arts projects or his collection of Sherlockiana. Said collection was the third largest still in private hands, and he was donating it all to St. Benignus—a big coup for a college our size. Some local corporations were putting up the money to maintain it.

Chalmers rose and shook my hand, exuding the sort of charm you'd expect from a guy who looked like a retired

British admiral. His skin was as soft as a baby's. He had a pleasant smile, showing teeth that were too perfect to be real.

"Delighted to meet you at last, young man," he said. "I've heard much about you from your admiring sister. I should very much like you to meet my wife." He leaned forward on the cane, looking toward a small knot of people at the other end of the living room, and raised his voice. "Renata?"

One of the women disengaged herself, flashed a brilliant smile at the group she was leaving, and joined our corner of the universe. Chalmers unnecessarily pronounced my name and his wife's.

"We've sort of already met," Renata Chalmers explained to her husband as she shook my hand.

"I'm afraid I drank most of that light beer you asked for," I said.

"No worries."

What the hell, then. I gulped down the rest of it.

Chapter Three
Night Work

Renata Chalmers had to be a good four decades younger than her husband and prettier than your average beauty queen. A cynic might look at the estimated girth of the old man's investment portfolio and draw conclusions, but whoever accused me of being a cynic?

"Jefferson is a cynic," my brother-in-law declared by way of further introduction. He stuck a long, green cigar in his mouth. In years gone by he would have fired it up with a lighter shaped like a hand grenade. Nowadays he mostly uses the cigar as a prop, yielding to Kate's no-smoking zone inside the house and sometimes to my protests about second-hand smoke outside of it.

"Why do you say that?" Renata asked.

"Because it is true," Mac said grandly. "Only a cynic—a man who knows the price of everything and the value of nothing, according to Oscar Wilde—could share Jefferson's total incomprehension of the joys of collecting."

I confessed that the passion to pay big money for things that nobody really needs, like multiple editions of the same Sherlock Holmes book and even variant printings of the same edition, was way beyond my ken.

"But maybe you can explain it," I told Chalmers. I whipped out my notebook and prepared for enlightenment. There could be a news release or an alumni mag article in this lunacy, which I would then tweet a link to.

"Think of it as a game," Chalmers said, leaning back on the couch, relaxed and in his element. "It's a chase that's always changing. Sometimes you know what you're looking for, but you don't know where to find it. Other times you know who has some unique item and the challenge is to make it yours. In Moscow, for example, I once talked a policeman out of a Russian first edition of *His Last Bow*."

"And you almost went to Lubyanka Prison or someplace equally awful on smuggling charges when you tried to take it out of the country," his wife reminded him.

Chalmers nodded at the memory. "There was no real crime involved, of course, except the extortion directed at me. Generous amounts of hard currency got me out of that pickle rather quickly. Overcoming obstacles—whether corrupt foreign officials or rival collectors—only adds zest to the game, Jeff."

Just thinking about it was enough to light the fire of battle in Chalmers's clear blue eyes.

"Oh, my collection isn't the largest," he went on, "but it is distinctive. No one else, for example, owns fully half the hand-written manuscript of *The Hound of the Baskervilles*."

I could imagine a nice photo spread of that, but why only half the MS? "Where's the rest of it?" I asked.

"Scattered," Chalmers said, "as it has been for more than a century. The manuscript was broken up and sent to book dealers as part of a promotion for the book's American publication in 1902. Various libraries and just a few private collectors own the other pages. One sold not so long ago for seventy-eight thousand dollars. Alas, I was not the purchaser."

"Then you obviously haven't been able to get everything you've gone after," I said.

Chalmers sat forward. His grip on the cane tightened. "Perhaps not, young man, but I always left the other fellow knowing he'd been in a fight. I play to win. Isn't that right, Renata?"

She nodded, her smile slipping a bit.

"And now you're just going to give away the Woollcott Chalmers Collection," I said. "I don't understand that part, either."

With an avuncular smile, Chalmers pointed his cane at Mac. "Blame your brother-in-law. He talked me into it."

Staying at a bed and breakfast in Savannah, Georgia, a couple of years back, I met a man who had once sold a refrigerator to an Eskimo in Alaska (who used it as a cigar humidor). Well, that guy had nothing on Sebastian McCabe when it comes to persuasion. But Mac refused the credit.

"Slander!" he thundered. "Calumny and character assassination! I talked you into nothing. I had heard that you were ready to share your collection, Woollcott, and I merely suggested that St. Benignus College would be a most grateful recipient."

Chalmers nodded. "True enough. There comes a time when hoarding it all to yourself is no longer satisfying. It becomes rather like Renata playing her violin to an empty concert hall or an actor performing to a darkened theater. Besides, after forty years the challenge has mostly disappeared. So I decided to give the collection away while I'm still alive to enjoy the gratitude—and the tax deduction."

"Perhaps Jefferson would enjoy a private tour of the exhibit right now," Mac rumbled.

The whole collection wasn't even unpacked yet, but some of the highlights were set up in a room next to the one where the speakers would be holding forth in the colloquium. Although I'd written about the exhibit in press releases and talked about it in pitching stories, I hadn't yet had a chance to see it. So I was mildly curious.

"But you can't just leave the party," I told Mac. "You're the host."

Mac looked at his watch, which had a silhouette of Sherlock Holmes on the face. "It is barely ten o'clock. With my charming wife presiding as hostess and ample adult beverages on hand to lubricate the guests, this jamboree will still be going strong long after we get back. We may not even be missed."

Further pro forma protests on my part proved predictably futile. Within ten minutes the four of us had piled into Mac's 1959 Chevy convertible, headed for Muckerheide Center on the St. Benignus campus. The car is fire-engine red with immense tail fins. It's no vehicle for a grown man at all, but it fits Sebastian McCabe just fine. Chalmers sat in front with Mac, apparently because it was easier on the older man's bum leg, and I sat in back next to Renata. She was a delightful conversationalist (although I can't remember a word she said—maybe something about her musical career) and she smelled so good I felt guilty just breathing around her.

A guard let us into Muckerheide Center, thanks to an advance call to Bobby Deere, who runs the center at night. The place was fully lighted, but eerily empty. The clicks of our heels on the tile floor echoed far down the wide corridors as we walked along.

On the first floor we passed the darkened offices, the abandoned Information Desk, and the empty racks that hold the campus newspaper when school is in session. Walking up the immobile escalator to the second level, Chalmers moved slowly, relying heavily on his cane. Just outside Hearth Room C, where the display from the Woollcott Chalmers Collection was set up behind closed doors, I realized we weren't going any farther without help.

"We need to get a key from that guard," I said in a near-whisper. The place had me a little spooked. "This baby's locked." By way of demonstration, I jiggled the handle. The door didn't move.

"No mere lock can stop Sebastian McCabe," my brother-in-law announced. He did not whisper. From his breast pocket he produced a yellow balloon. "Be so good as to blow this up, please," he asked Renata Chalmers as he handed it to her. She hesitated, clearly bewildered by Mac's madcap actions. Apparently she didn't know him very well.

"Humor him," I said as Mac lit a cigar. "You may have children of your own some day."

Looking resigned rather than enthusiastic, she blew up the balloon. Her husband, at Mac's request, tied the balloon shut and handed it over to Mac—who immediately applied the hot tip of his cigar to the latex. The balloon popped and something clattered to the floor. Renata picked it up and handed it to Mac—an old-fashioned metal key.

"I believe this will facilitate our entrance," Mac said.

Woollcott Chalmers tucked his cane under his right arm and clapped softly in appreciation of this sophomoric parlor trick. "Bravo!" His wife smiled, the rough equivalent of turning on a mega-watt spotlight.

"Can't you ever do anything the easy way?" I asked Mac.

"What would be the fun of that, old boy?"

He used the key to open the door. At first he fumbled for a light switch, then found it on the wall to his left. The fluorescent tubes on the ceiling blinked on with the flickering brightness of lightning.

The Chalmers Collection filled the room, some of it spread out on tables, some on the walls, some in bookcases. There were books, posters, calendars, records—anything to which the name or image of Sherlock Holmes had been applied. It was hard to take it all in. And this was only a small sampling of the collection; the bulk of it remained in packing boxes over at the library.

"Incredible," I said. "I've never seen anything like it."

"Nor will you," Chalmers assured me. "There is nothing like it. Perhaps that is immodest, but as Holmes once said, 'I cannot agree with those who rank modesty among the virtues.'"

He watched in silence from the doorway as the rest of us strolled through the room. Mac dawdled over some faded paperbacks, the particular kind of book toward which his own collection mania is bent. I got caught up in the bizarre design of a Firesign Theatre record album called "The Giant Rat of Sumatra."

"Don't waste your time with that," Chalmers said when he saw what I was up to. He pointed with his cane to a glass case against the far wall. "There lay the real gems of my forty years of collecting Sherlockiana."

I put the album down and joined Mac and Renata in following Chalmers across the room.

The case to which the collector had pointed was lined in red velvet, giving it the air of a reliquary. Reposing on the cloth were several letters, a calling card from Arthur Conan Doyle with a note scribbled on it, a small playbill from an early performance of the melodrama *Sherlock Holmes* signed by the lead actor, William Gillette, and several books whose bibliographical significance escaped me.

Chalmers said, "Until I found it, no one even suspected the existence of—"

"Woollcott!"

Renata, grabbing his arm tightly, didn't need to say anything else. Chalmers's blue eyes, magnified by his thick glasses, grew even wider as he instantly saw what his wife was too flustered to voice.

"I don't—" He hesitated, shaking his head. "I can't believe it. This afternoon . . . everything was here when we left."

His wife nodded. "I know."

"What is it?" Mac asked sharply. "What's missing?"

"The *Hound of the Baskervilles* manuscript," Renata replied.

"Much more than that," Chalmers added in an agitated voice. "There was also a first edition of the *Hound* inscribed by Conan Doyle to Fletcher Robinson himself. And a *Beeton's Christmas Annual* of 1887, the rarest of all Sherlockian books, made even rarer by a hand-written note on the first page from Conan Doyle to his mother."

I whistled. "That kind of stuff must be worth a pretty penny."

"Priceless!" Mac thundered. He tugged on his beard. "I find it hard to credit that our librarian misplaced them."

"There's no chance of that," Renata said. "They were here when we left this afternoon after helping set up the display. They've been stolen."

Chapter Four
"We've Had a Little Incident"

"And it's only my first month on the job," Gene Pfannenstiel moaned, shaking his shaggy head.

"I know," I told the young librarian.

"Nothing like this ever happened anywhere else I've worked," he assured me.

"You said that already," I reminded him. "Twice."

Gene's broad face, usually alive with the excitement of some bookish pursuit that would have put me to sleep, was a study in earnest concern. Or as earnest as a chunky man can look in a frizzy beard and no mustache.

In pleated black slacks and a white shirt open at the collar, he was dressed more like an Amish storekeeper than the curator of special collections at the Lee J. Bennish Memorial Library. Blinking around at the rest of us, he looked about as worldly, too.

"I should have asked to have special guards posted outside," he fretted.

"That's obvious," said Lieutenant Ed Decker of Campus Security.

"Not particularly helpful at this juncture, however," Mac rumbled.

By this time he had driven Woollcott and Renata Chalmers back to the McCabe house, where they were staying the weekend. The old man had left looking about ten years older.

I wasn't feeling so hot myself. It didn't take a public relations genius to figure that news of the Sherlockian thefts would quickly overshadow everything else happening on campus this weekend. A major gift to the college—or parts of it, anyway—had been stolen almost as soon as the collection had arrived. That made us look like a bunch of rubes. Plus there was the Holmes connection, guaranteed to set off a media feeding frenzy. Dealing with the press would be a headache on this one, and that was the least of my worries. A certain unbearable college administrator was sure to make my life really miserable.

The facts of the theft were not in doubt: Both of the Chalmerses and Gene Pfannenstiel agreed that the missing materials had been in the glass case before Gene locked up the room that afternoon in front of the couple. With much hocus-pocus Mac had unlocked the room many hours later using the same key, borrowed from Gene. In between, something had happened.

"Grand theft," Decker pronounced unnecessarily. "I understand the stolen goods were worth way into five figures, maybe six. Right?"

Mac shrugged his shoulders, which is akin to a mountain moving. "How does one assess the value of something that is one of a kind?"

"And Mr. Pfannenstiel here simply gave you the key, Professor? How do you rate such treatment?"

From the look on his face, the question worried Gene, but not Mac. "Rank has its privileges, Lieutenant," he said, "and I am a full professor well known to the library staff."

"Damned sloppy security," Decker said with a snort. "The display case wasn't even locked." He glared at Gene, who withered under the attention and didn't bother to explain that he hadn't thought that to be necessary in a room that was itself locked.

Decker looked mean. But then, Decker always looks mean, even when he hasn't been hauled into work late on a Friday evening. He's built like one of those beefy football players whose jersey number, according to legend, is higher than his IQ. So you probably expect me to say he's really a heck of a nice guy and a Rhodes scholars on top of it. Not quite. Oh, he's cooperative enough—letting me know routinely about requests for demonstration permits, for example, so I can be prepared to respond for the media. But Decker is no genius, just a thoroughly professional police officer with skin the color of anthracite, a broad flat nose, a thin mustache, high cheek bones and arms the size of Mac's thighs.

"I already have a list and description of what Mr. Chalmers knows was taken," Decker said, tapping a small notebook in his hand, "but I'll need you to do a complete inventory, Mr. Pfannenstiel, to make sure nothing else is missing."

"Right away, Lieutenant."

"Good. Anything else I need to know?"

"Yes!" Mac thundered. "I call your attention to what Sherlock Holmes might have called the curious incident of the broken lock."

"But the lock wasn't broken," Decker protested.

"That was the curious incident. How did our burglar get in there without breaking the lock?"

"You tell us," I snapped. "You're the magician."

Mac slowly shook his massive head. "I have no special insight. Houdini could get into places as well as out of them, but most often he had the help of a concealed lock pick. When you examine the lock, as I did before the lieutenant arrived, you will notice there are virtually no scratches around the lock. It is difficult, if not impossible, to use a lock pick without making scratches."

Muttering something under his breath (I distinctly caught the phrase "frickin' amateurs"), Decker went off to direct two newly arrived officers in dusting for fingerprints or whatever it is cops do at a crime scene.

"I can't put if off any longer," I told Mac. "I've got to call Ralph."

"You have my deepest sympathy."

I didn't want to do this in front of an audience, so I walked over to the other side of the escalator before I pulled out my iPhone and selected the number in my contacts list I'd been dreading to call.

Ralph Pendergast is vice president of academic affairs and provost at St. Benignus College, which makes him both Mac's boss and mine. That's dicey enough. But on top of that, his strong ties to several members of the college's board of trustees make him almost as powerful in every facet of college life as our legendary president, Father Joseph F. Pirelli, C.T.L.—"Father Joe"—himself. And yet Ralph is relatively new to campus, brought in by the board just this academic year to tighten up the ship.

The guiding dream of Ralph's life seems to be a campus where nothing out of the mainstream is ever taught, nothing controversial ever happens, and the bottom line is always written in black ink. I bet his favorite flavor of ice cream is vanilla. No surprise, then, that *The Write Stuff*, Mac's blog nitpicking the grammatical foibles in faculty and staff writing on our campus—including Ralph's administrative memos—sent Ralph's blood pressure off the charts. Mac's other eccentricities, such as his penchant for bagpipes and his success in writing mystery novels, only rubbed salt in the wound.

Ralph Pendergast, let me make clear, does not like Sebastian McCabe. He also does not like me because of my inability to keep Mac's escapades out of the local press. And he absolutely hates surprises, which is why I was calling him with the bad news at this hour instead of letting him find out in the morning from the stories I was almost certain would appear in our local media.

He picked up the phone on the fifth ring, his voice groggy. Early to bed, early to rise.

"Sorry to wake you, Ralph," I said. "This is Jeff Cody."

"Cody? Oh, no."

"Yes, sir. We've had a little incident you should know about." I quickly outlined the situation.

"This is a disaster," Ralph announced. "Simply a disaster." I could imagine him pressing together his thin lips, running a hand through his slicked-back hair, maybe fumbling at his bedside for his wire-rimmed glasses. "I personally secured the corporate sponsors for this Chalmers Collection. Do you have any idea what this theft will do to our reputation in the business community?"

It wasn't really a question.

I looked across the way. Mac was standing outside the exhibit room, next to the NO SMOKING sign, smoking a cigar.

"I should have known better than to let myself become involved in any McCabe project," Ralph continued. "Sherlock Holmes, indeed!"

"You can hardly blame Mac this time," I pointed out, grudgingly, out of my irrepressible sense of fairness. "As academic vice president, you're in charge of the damned library. If your curator of special collections had taken some precautions—"

Why was I throwing Gene under the bus like that?

"Don't let them play it cute," Ralph interrupted.

"What?"

"The media. Don't let them say it's another case for Sherlock Holmes or something like that. They'll put that on the front page. Get them to play it straight."

"The media aren't the enemy here, Ralph." *You are.* "The best way to handle a public relations crisis is to be as open and accurate and responsive with the media as you can. If you've made a mistake, admit it and apologize. Have a bad day, if necessary, and get it behind you, move on."

"We didn't make a mistake. Don't make this about the college. How the media choose to cover this is the issue."

I took a deep breath. "Get real, Ralph. There's no way I can tell the media how to play a story."

"Then what good are you? And I was certainly under the impression that you had . . . connections, shall we say, at the *Observer*."

"Don't get personal, Ralph. Besides, that's all over."

"Emphasize the law enforcement angle," Ralph went on, ignoring me as usual. "Campus Security is on the case, near a solution, that sort of thing."

I barely heard him. On the other side of the escalator a stocky man in his mid-fifties, dressed in a dapper twill suit, was sidling up to my brother-in-law.

"Okay, Ralph," I blurted into the phone, "I'll take care of it. If you get any media calls, send them to me. But I have to go now. The press is already on the scene."

Chapter Five
"Someone I Know"

Even at eleven o'clock at night, Bernard J. Silverstein was impeccably attired in a crisp white shirt and freshly pressed three-piece suit. He looked, as always, more like a professor than a news hawk. He also looked more like a professor than the professors.

"Hello, Jeff," he said. "Interesting caper somebody pulled here."

"I prefer to think of it as an incident, Ben. You pick it up on the police scanner?" Ben writes about police, courts, aviation and restaurants for the *Erin Observer & News Ledger*. In the summer he also writes a gardening column.

"Uh-huh." Ben pulled a gnarled black pipe out of his coat pocket and stuck it between his thick lips without lighting it. "So what happened?"

Mac took the cigar out of his mouth, as if to speak.

"That's what Campus Security is trying to determine now," I interjected before my brother-in-law could talk.

"Don't hand me that line of bovine excrement," Jeff," Ben said. He blinked his owlish eyes. "You know I need some information and I need it fast for the website. That's the tail that wags the dog now."

Nearly forty years in the journalistic backwaters had turned Ben Silverstein's curly hair an iron gray. Two heart attacks had convinced him to modify his bull-terrier approach to getting a story, but he was still a real newsman—one of the best I'd ever known.

"Let me talk to Decker and find out what he's learned," I said.

"I'd rather talk to him myself."

"No doubt."

"The lieutenant ejected me rather unceremoniously from the crime scene," Mac complained.

"Good," I said. "Let me get back to you, Ben."

Decker was drinking machine-brewed coffee out of a paper cup as he watched his men (one of whom was a woman) take photos and draw sketches of the scene.

"Your favorite press hound is yapping at my heels," I told him. "What kind of bone can I throw the man?"

"It's okay to give out the titles and descriptions of the stuff that was stolen," Decker said. "The estimated value, such as it is, is useable. And you can say means of entry is unknown. But don't make a big deal out of that. If by any chance McCabe is right, that could be an important clue and I don't want to tip off the thief that we're on to it. Oh, and the crime had to have taken place between five this afternoon and the time you folks came. I guess that's it. Thanks for handling Silverstein, Jeff."

Out in the corridor again, I gave Ben everything I had from Decker, plus some details from my own knowledge of how the theft was discovered.

"This heinous crime will not go long unsolved," Mac vowed.

"I suppose not," Ben said, looking up from his notebook, "what with all these—what do you call them?— these Sherlockians around here for the next couple of days."

Ralph's worst fear. I sighed. "I was really hoping you wouldn't get carried away with that, Ben. I mean, I'm sure that Decker's troops will find the thief in due course. This Sherlock Holmes angle is really kind of a sideshow, a distraction to the real news here."

Ben snorted. "The Sherlock Holmes angle *is* the news, my lad. You wanted to be a reporter once, if I can remember back nearly twenty years when you were working on the campus paper. Tell me the truth: Would you soft pedal the Holmes stuff if you were writing this story?"

Instead of answering that, I said, "Well, you know I had to try."

Ben's mouth formed a grin around his unlit pipe. "Besides, my editor wouldn't let me take a pass on the fun part. Aren't you going to ask how she is?"

Lynda Teal, news editor of the *Erin Observer & News Ledger*, had been my girlfriend for four years. Had been, that is, until about a month back when she had declared her independence from what she considered my possessiveness and nagging. Nagging, she called it—just because I frequently provided her with helpful information about the dangers of cigarette smoking. I was only telling her for her own good, wasn't I? Well, all right, maybe our relationship problems went a tad deeper than that. I still haven't figured out why she called me a tall Woody Allen.

So now her Facebook profile said "Single" instead of "In a relationship with Jeff Cody." At least I hadn't been replaced yet. I keep checking.She hadn't de-friended me, either. There was hope in that.

"No," I told Ben, "I don't think I'm going to ask how she is."

"Well, she's fine. Just fine."

"Glad to hear it."

After the stocky reporter left, Mac said, "Bernard is quite right, you know."

"He must be," I said bitterly. "Everybody else says the same thing. I can't walk down Main Street without meeting somebody who wants to tell me how well Lynda's doing without me."

"Not about that. On Ms. Teal's well-being I have no data, and thus no conclusion. I refer to his assertion that our Sherlockian friends are central to this crime."

"How do you figure that?" I asked with a sinking feeling.

"You don't believe the stolen collectibles could be fenced through normal channels, do you? Of course not. They are too highly specialized. Whoever took them either wanted them for himself or already had a collector lined up to purchase them. In either case, the thief was knowledgeable enough to pick the most valuable items— items that had not been singled out in press accounts of the collection. Ergo, he or she is a Sherlockian. The odds are astronomical that the person in question will be at the colloquium tomorrow. Quite likely, it is even someone I know."

INVESTIGATING
ARTHUR CONAN DOYLE
AND
SHERLOCK HOLMES

A Colloquium

St. Benignus College
Erin, Ohio
March 12–13, 2011

Sessions in Hearth Room, A and B
Herman J. Muckerheide Center
(except as otherwise noted)

Saturday, March 12

Session One

9:00   Registration outside Hearth Room
       Coffee and Danish
       "Field Bazaar" selling Sherlockiana

10:00 Orientation—Dr. Sebastian McCabe,
       BSI,St. Benignus College

10:15 Movietone Interview / Arthur Conan Doyle

10:30 "Sherlock Holmes and the Development of
       the Detective Story"—Mr. Al Kane,
       Sarasota, Florida

11:00 "CollectingSherlockiana"—Mr. Woollcott
       Chalmers, BSI, Cincinnati, Ohio

11:45 Sherlockian Quiz

Noon   Lunch (President's Dining Room)
       Opportunity to visit selections from the
       Chalmers Collection (Hearth Room, C)

1:00   Presentation of the Woollcott Chalmers
       Collection to St. Benignus College (Hearth
       Room C)

Chapter Six
"A Most Valuable Institution"

When I woke up the next morning I soon wished I hadn't. Lack of adequate sleep always gives me a headache to start the day, but not as big as the one I got from looking at the front page of the *Erin Observer & News Ledger*.

In the hubbub the night before, I'd forgotten to check out the online version of Ben Silverstein's story on the paper's website, so I was coming at it cold. It was set apart in a box at the top right of the page with a three-column headline, thirty-six-point type, bold face: **A CASE FOR SHERLOCK HOLMES**.

Damn. Ralph would blow whatever gaskets he had left.

"This is looking like a case for Sherlock Holmes," Ben's piece began, grabbing the obvious hook for the lead.

"A manuscript and two valuable books from the famed Woollcott Chalmers Collection of Holmes materials were stolen Friday from a temporary display on the St. Benignus College campus.

"College spokesman T. Jefferson Cody said the value of the collection . . ."

The Indiana Jones theme song blaring from my night-stand stopped me there. It was the ring tone on my iPhone. Morrie Kindle, the Associated Press stringer, was calling to confirm the details of the *Observer* story. I read through the rest of it in a hurry, told him it was correct, and promised to get back to him if there were anything new from Campus Security. I called Decker's office, but he wasn't in yet. I knew he would be eventually, Saturday or not.

This was just the beginning, I realized with a sense of doom as I left my apartment. Once Kindle's rewrite of the story hit the AP feed, calls would be coming in from all over the map. No time to worry about that, though. I had to go show the flag at the colloquium, plus be on hand to help a TV reporter shoot a few sound bites in the late morning.

My carriage house apartment next to Mac's house, seventeen steps above his garage, is only a ten-minute bicycle ride from campus. I picked up my Schwinn and pedaled off, all the while imagining Ralph's reaction to Ben's story. It didn't take much imagination.

A registration table was set up outside of Hearth Rooms A and B. AneliesePokorny, my diminutive administrative assistant, was taking money and handing out name tags. Popcorn is forty-nine years old, dyes her hair blond, and would cheerfully commit grand theft auto if Mac asked her to. She was volunteering her time this morning. I greeted her while the guy in front of me handed over a designer check carrying a silhouette of Sherlock Holmes.

"Do you feel as bad as you look?" she asked.

"Worse."

Popcorn gave me a nametag with my moniker already typed in. I pinned it on, poured myself a cup of decaf from the coffee-and-pastries spread next to her, then went to survey the scene.

Hearth Room C, the scene of last night's excitement, was sealed off by Decker's men with yellow plastic tape. Immediately to the left was the door to Room B, which functioned as the entrance to the back of the Hearth Room when Aand B were opened up to form one hall as they were today. I went in that way, intending to stay at the back of the room for a good view of the crowd and an unobtrusive exit when necessary.

It was about ten minutes until show time and the place was filling up. Maybe fifty or sixty people were there so far out of seventy-eight registered in advance and a few walk-ins expected. I counted six deerstalker caps. Mac and the Chalmerses were in the middle of the room, fiddling with a laptop and projector setup. I also noticed Al Kane, author turned pitchman; Dr. Noah Queensbury, the bore with Basil Rathbone's nose; and a few others from Mac's party that I couldn't put a name to. One was a handsome, slightly plump woman with gray-blond hair who'd been in the kitchen the night before talking about Dr. Watson.

If Mac was right—and I didn't doubt it—whoever stole those books yesterday was probably in this room right now.

I sipped my decaf and found myself turned toward the back of the room. A series of tables running the length of the far wall were covered with Sherlockian bric-a-brac for sale from a handful of vendors. There was a ton of books, of course, but also a lot more—drinking glasses, book bags, Christmas ornaments, buttons ("HOLMES IS WHERE THE ♥ IS," "HOLMES SWEET HOLMES"), tie tacks, posters, CDs, DVDs, computer games, board games, and T-shirts. There were even a few deerstalker caps on the end of the table where a hairless man in a bow tie was accepting money from people buying these treasures. This was the "field bazaar," according to the colloquium program. I was just thinking that somebody had misspelled "bizarre" when I heard an all-too-familiar rumble behind me.

"Rather impressive for our first colloquium, eh, Jefferson?"

I whirled around, nearly spilling my coffee, just in time to see my brother-in-law bite into a pastry with some sort of white filling that oozed out of both sides of his mouth.

"That wasn't really the word I had in mind," I said.

I was spared elaboration by the arrival of Al Kane, who appeared behind Mac looking like a hung-over CPA. He must have made a few too many assaults on the liquid provisions at Mac's house last night. His mustache was crooked, the evident result of an unsteady hand with the razor, and his breath smelled like cigarettes.

"I hear somebody made a big score yesterday," he rasped.

"You refer, of course, to the raid on the Chalmers Collection?" Mac said. We hadn't mentioned it last night upon sneaking back into his house because Mac didn't want to put a damper on what remained of the party.

Kane nodded. "Sure."

"Is everybody talking about it already?" I asked, exasperated.

"Everyone," Mac assured me happily.

Great.

"It's in the *Erin* newspaper this morning," Dr. Queensbury said unnecessarily, joining us. "'The press, Watson, is a most valuable institution, if only you know how to use it.'—'The Adventure of the Six Napoleons.' It is rather exciting, don't you think? A real Sherlock Holmes mystery."

Queensbury had "BSI" after his name on the colloquium program, the same as Mac, meaning that he was a member of the Baker Street Irregulars. That's a big deal for American Sherlockians, and maybe why he felt compelled to quote the Sacred Writings of the cult. *At least the "BS" part fits.*

I looked around, straining my eyeballs for a familiar face. Surely the *Observer* would send somebody to follow up on Ben's story, probably Maggie Barton. The old gal covers the college most of the time, except for the occasional campus crime story that went to Ben Silverstein, and she'd written a couple of advance stories about the colloquium and the donation of the Chalmers Collection. But I didn't catch a glimpse of her.

"Certainly this is a prime opportunity for a display of Sherlockian deduction," Mac said. "Or induction, to be accurate but uncanonical."

Al Kane snorted. "Play Holmes, you mean? Solve the crime like an amateur sleuth in some book? Forget it, Mac. It's never happened and it never will. Put the whole lot of you against one professional police officer with a crime lab behind him and it's no contest."

"He's right, you know," I said for the benefit of Mac and Queensbury and a few others hanging at the periphery of the conversation. "Maybe Max Cutter or Red Maddox could use force to find out a few things the cops can't because the boys in blue are hemmed in by Miranda rules and the rights of criminals. But a modern-day Sherlock Holmes just wouldn't cut it."

"Cynics," Mac said.

"Okay, then," Kane said, "just how would you use Sherlockian methods to solve this adventure of the rare book thefts?"

"Holmes would never be called in," Queensbury asserted, not waiting for Mac to answer. "The case isn't unusual enough. No red-headed league, no apparent madman destroying statues of Napoleon, no mysterious speckled band—"

"That," said Mac, "begs the issue. The real question is, what *are* the methods of Sherlock Holmes? Holmes always observed the trifles, of course, and deduced—or induced—from them. He also employed street urchins, special knowledge, instinct, logic, legwork, disguise, burglary, subterfuge, process of elimination, science, dogs, advertising, analogy to similar cases and—oh, yes— prodigious amounts of tobacco."

He pulled out a cigar. "Personally, I intend to rely heavily upon the latter."

"You intend?" With dismay I heard my own voice came out as an incredulous screech.

"Of course, Jefferson. It can hardly have escaped you that I intend to solve this case. I will, of course, use Damon Devlin's techniques as well as those of Sherlock Holmes."

He snapped his fingers, creating a flame he used to light his cigar seemingly right off his fingertips. It was just the sort of stunt his damned magician-sleuth was always pulling in Mac's books. How long, I wondered, had he waited for just the right moment to do that?

"Are you serious?" Kane asked before I could lodge a protest that this was a non-smoking public building (not that he really intended to smoke—he was just showing off).

"Why should I be otherwise?" Mac asked. "If I can create fictional mysteries in such abundance, surely I can solve a real one. You well know that mysteries, whether physical or metaphysical, are my métier, my forte, my meat and—"

"Yeah, yeah," I agreed, shutting off the *Roget's Thesaurus* monologue. "But I still say my Max Cutter could beat the pants off Sherlock Holmes."

"We shall see," Mac said, eyeing his Sherlock Holmes watch. "Not at the moment, however. The time has come to begin the colloquium."

He moved like a cruise liner toward the front of the room while I seated myself on a couch near the rear, with Kane next to me. Kane pointed toward Chalmers, who was taking a chair in the front row, the radiant Renata at his side.

"If this were my book, he'd be my man," Kane confided in a low voice.

"You mean the old insurance scam?" I said. "That wouldn't work—he's already signed over the whole collection to St. Benignus. You can't insure something you don't own anymore."

"That's not what I had in mind, Cody. Look, Chalmers picked up a sweet tax deduction by donating all that stuff to your college. But suppose he realized afterward there were a few precious items he just couldn't live without. He could have stolen them back to gloat over in private. Best of all possible worlds for him—tax deduction and he still keeps the books. That's how Red Maddox would figure it, anyway."

This wasn't a Red Maddox mystery story by a long shot.

But that didn't mean Red's creator wasn't on to something.

Chapter Seven
"We Have to Talk"

I stared at Chalmers for a while, musing over Kane's idea. Then my eyes slid over and I was looking at his wife. It was hard not to. She was dressed in a gray pinstriped double-breasted suit, pants included, and a white blouse. The outfit could have been stolen from Al Capone. I don't know whether it was out of style or so old it was new again, but she certainly filled it out nicely. Her black hair was gathered behind her head in a simple red ribbon.

"I see Renata's charms aren't lost on you," came a feminine whisper in my ear.

I gave a guilty start and turned around to see my sister, Kate, sitting in a chair next to the couch I occupied. Just like her to sneak up on me like that.

"I was looking at her leather handbag," I lied. "Look at how big that baby is. I've seen suitcases smaller."

"R-i-g-h-t. That lady is strong medicine. Better watch yourself, T.J."

"I'd rather watch her."

Actually, I'm old enough to have figured out a long time ago that it's not a good idea to covet thy neighbor's wife—or anybody else's. I'd seen too many people lose too much that way. I was a free agent, not by choice, but Mrs. Chalmers wasn't. I didn't give Big Sister the satisfaction of verbalizing that to her, however.

"Tell me about her," I said. "Who is she, besides Mrs. Woollcott Chalmers?"

"She's a very smart lady, and very talented—aclassical violinist with the Cincinnati Symphony Orchestra. She also runs an arts center, which is where she met Woollcott. He was a board member and a widower."

"Did he pursue her or did she pursue him?" Idle curiosity.

"Shhhh," said Kate, the person who had initiated the whole conversation. Mac was at the lectern now, in his element. Except for his beard, he looked almost Churchillian: stout, a few inches below my height, dressed in a tweed suit and bow tie, master of all he surveyed. He winked at my sister, put on his glasses to read his notes, and bellowed:

"'Come, Watson, come! The game is afoot!' If those familiar words lift your spirits and gladden your hearts, ladies and gentlemen, you have come to the right place. Welcome to the first annual 'Investigating Arthur Conan Doyle and Sherlock Holmes' colloquium."

"ACD/SH Colloquium underway," I tweeted from my iPhone.

I looked around as Mac talked on. A few people were already dressed for the Victorian costume contest to be held that evening—a man in a derby, for instance, and a woman wearing a white dress, a straw hat, and a VOTE FOR WOMEN banner across her ample bosom. Bob Nakamora, the camera-toting Japanese-American from Mac's party the night before, wore a sweatshirt with a drawing of Sherlock Holmes on the front. Just as he put the Nikon up to his face to take a picture, a flash went off to my right. Somebody was taking a picture of Bob taking a picture. I looked over and saw, to my surprise, Lynda Teal behind the camera.

She was dressed in a short tan skirt and a red blouse. Black and silver earrings matched the buckle on her black belt. Her hair, naturally curly and the color of dark honey, was chin length, a little longer than I was used to seeing it.

Not that I noticed. I looked away and pulled my mind back to Mac's spiel.

"It's no surprise that Holmes was a commanding figure in his own age, the late Victorian," he was lecturing. "The Great Detective was above all a man of logic and science at a time when science seemed to have all the answers, not just more questions. He battled speckled bands and hounds from hell with only the faithful Watson at his side—and yes, he nearly always won. Today, however, the world faces far more frightening monsters, man-made creations of our laboratories and bomb factories. How do we explain the continued popularity of Mr. Sherlock Holmes of Baker Street in these jaded and dangerous times?

"Could it be that Holmes is hero and father figure in a period that sorely needs both? Even though Holmes sometimes fails he is always a reassuring presence. When he is around we feel that everything is all right. And, of course, Holmes is always there when we need him, never farther away than a wire to summon him and a train to get him there. For these reasons and many more, we must agree with Sir Arthur Conan Doyle's brother-in-law, E.W. Hornung, who so famously said, 'Though he might be more humble, there's no police like Holmes.'"

I groaned inwardly as the Sherlockians chuckled. So, I thought, Conan Doyle had to put up with a brother-in-law, too. I felt his pain.

Just then Lynda walked past, apparently not seeing me, and grabbed an empty seat about three rows away. I watched her strike up a conversation with the man next to her—early forties, light brown hair, tanned skin, professional smile and a Rolex watch. He looked like he'd gotten lost on his way to the cover of *GQ*. As they chatted, Lynda pulled out her notebook.

"Who's the guy Lynda's talking to?" I whispered to Kate.

"You mean the hunk?"

Muscles fairly rippled beneath his cashmere sweater.

"I don't think he's such a hunk," I said. "Who the hell is he?"

"Hugh Matheson. The attorney."

Further identification would have been superfluous. Hugh Matheson was one of the most famous litigators in the country. He hung his hat in Cincinnati, but he traveled everywhere. His shtick was a legal theory called "hedonic damages." In English, that means he made his bread and butter—and probably a yacht or two—convincing juries to base damage awards on the "missed joy of life" rather than on some concrete fact such as lost wages. The joy of life turned out to be quite expensive for companies that had the ill fortune to face Matheson in a court room. *60 Minutes* had recently estimated his personal worth at forty million dollars—even after hefty alimony payments to wives numbers one through three. There was no number four yet.

At least he was shorter than me.

"What's he doing here?" I asked Kate.

"He's a Sherlockian, of course, a member of the Anglo-Indian Club. And a collector. He and Woollcott don't get along at all."

"Unfriendly rivals, eh?" I could readily imagine Chalmers, in pursuit of bookish rarities, following a scorched earth policy not designed to win friends and influence people.

In front of us, Lynda looked around the room as if to get a handle on how many people were there. Her eye caught mine and her mouth spread in a smile of recognition. She waved. My heart skipped a beat and the blood pounded in my ears as if I were a teenager. This was ridiculous.

Instead of waving back, I turned to my sister. "Then Matheson probably isn't too broken up about what happened to the Chalmers Collection last night."

"I suppose not," Kate said, "but you'd never get a collector to admit a thing like that."

At the front of the room Mac yielded to an old video of Sir Arthur Conan Doyle talking about how he had come to create Sherlock Holmes. The gist of it was that he had intended Holmes to be different from the fictional sleuths of his day who solved their cases without showing how they had arrived at the solutions. Surprisingly, he spoke in a soft Scottish burr that reminded me of Sean Connery in *Indiana Jones and the Last Crusade*.

The atmosphere in the Hearth Room was more casual and less reverent than I'd expected. Some Sherlockians talked quietly among themselves or fiddled with smartphones all through the video, perhaps having seen it before. Others looked through books and trinkets at the back of the room. In a wingback chair behind me a woman knitted. A guy sitting on the floor next to her crunched Ruffles potato chips. Hugh Matheson leaned over and said something to Lynda, who giggled. I swear the woman giggled.

The film ended, the lights went up, and Mac took the floor again to introduce Al Kane. I checked my watch: ten-thirty. The program was running right on schedule and I had fifteen minutes before I had to meet the reporter from Channel 4 Action News.

As he followed the massive McCabe to the lectern, peering at his audience through wire-rimmed glasses as if in apprehension, Kane looked less hard-boiled than ever. Only the obvious hangover put me in mind of his Red Maddox character.

"Of course, Edgar Allen Poe invented the detective story—and almost every significant convention of the craft still used and misused today," he began. "It was Arthur Conan Doyle, however, who gave the form universal and timeless appeal."

Kane described how Conan Doyle had improved on the formula developed in Poe's three detective stories plus

"The Gold-Bug" by making the endings sharper and the narrator more of a character.

I found myself mentally wandering back to Kane's casual comment about Woollcott Chalmers himself as a suspect in yesterday's thefts.

How would my Max Cutter figure it? Chalmers was hardly spry enough to do the deed himself, but that was no reason to rule out a man with his money and his determination.He could pay to have it done. But the risk was all out of proportion to the reward. The stolen books and manuscript pages may have been worth who-knows-what, but they were only three items out of thousands he had given away in the Woollcott Chalmers Collection. Would Chalmers have let himself in for a grand theft rap just because he couldn't part with that particular trio of goodies? Maybe so, but the Max Cutter inside me couldn't buy it.

"Holmes is an urban creature, although he does sometimes don the deerstalker and venture into the countryside," Kane continued from the podium. "He is a loner, often cutting even Watson out of the loop. He has no permanent lady except the faithful Mrs. Hudson. He often operates outside the law, committing burglary in four stories and several times letting the villain flee—or die. He bucks authority, even royalty, and he can't be bought. All are characteristics of the hard-boiled detective, from the earliest heroes of *Black Mask* magazine down to a fellow I know named Red Maddox."

"Hard-boiled Holmes?" I tweeted. *"So says Al Kane."*

I looked at my watch again. Damn, the TV crew was due in five minutes. "Cutting out," I whispered to Kate. She nodded and I went out the door next to the woman who was knitting.

The corridor was empty, except for Popcorn reading a book as she sat alone at the registration table. She looked up and gave a little wave, then went back to reading *Love's Savage Desire*.

I don't know why I had entertained a fear the TV people would be early; it would be a minor miracle if they were no more than ten minutes late.

Al Kane's talk, amplified over the wall speakers, permeated the air outside the Hearth Room like the voice of God. But soon it was cut through by another voice there in the corridor, a husky one a bit like Lauren Bacall in *The Big Sleep*.

"Jeff!" she called.

I whirled around.

"We have to talk," Lynda said.

Chapter Eight
Out of Control

The impact of Lynda Teal's gaze—those wide, brown eyes flecked with gold—is one of the strongest natural forces known to mankind. Only with great effort did I withstand the soulful expression she laid on me.

"I thought you'd send Maggie Barton," I blurted out.

"Sorry to disappoint you," Lynda said. "Maggie broke her ankle in a parachuting accident. You know Ben worked late last night. I didn't have anybody else to send but me."

Maggie Barton is almost seventy and has hair the color and consistency of pink cotton candy. I made a mental note to send her a get-well card.

"I'm very sorry, Ms. Teal," I said coolly, "but if you want to ask about the theft yesterday I don't have anything to add to what I told Ben Silverstein last night. I'd be glad to get back to you, though, after I talk to Campus Security."

"That's not what this is about and you know it." She did not actually add an unladylike "a-hole," but that was implied. "I want to discuss *us.*" Did I mention that her throaty voice drives me wild?

"Ms. Teal, there is no *us*," I said with determined reserve. "You made that quite clear four weeks and two days ago." *Not that I've been counting.*

"Damn it, quit calling me Ms. Teal! I want us to still be friends."

I didn't think she meant "with privileges." I'd heard this tune before, back when she'd given me the old heave-ho the previous month. I hadn't seen her much since, but I'd never stopped thinking about her.

"Of course we're friends." I smiled like a politician while my stomach did gymnastics. This wasn't going well.

"Like hell we are! You've been avoiding me ever since we broke up, Jeff."

"I distinctly remember that it wasn't my idea to stop seeing each other."

She threw up her hands. "If you hadn't been so controlling, so self-righteous, so neurotic—" Lynda is half-Italian and sometimes expressive.

"Excuse me," I said, cutting off the litany of my finer points as I moved away from her. "I have to deal with the broadcast media."

The team from TV4 Action News had just appeared at the top of the escalator. *Saved by the bell.*

"You're not getting off the hook that easily, Jeff Cody," Lynda called after me. "I'm going to be here all weekend!"

The photographer sent by the Cincinnati TV station was an old hand named Sam Gardner who seemed to have taken on a permanent lean from thirty years of lugging television cameras, starting when they were a lot heavier than they are now. He'd acquired other baggage as well—a heavy dose of gray in his hair, a perpetual scowl on his ebony face, and a cynical outlook on the world at large. He was known in the trade as Smiling Sam. I liked him.

"New intern for you, Cody," he said without bothering to look at me. "You can break her in." Knowing Sam, I didn't think the smutty double meaning was an accident.

She said her name was Mandy Petrowski but she was thinking of changing it to Preston or Peters or Prescott and what did I think?

I thought she should change the Mandy, but I said, "On you, Petrowski works just fine."

She flashed me a smile without a hint of a flirt in it. I felt ancient.

Mandy was no more than twenty-two and a senior at Miami University in Oxford, Ohio. But she seemed to have all the right ingredients for a career in TV journalism—lush auburn hair done up in anchorwoman style, perfect teeth, a generous mouth, a cute nose, a clear-channel voice devoid of accent, and a Saks Fifth Avenue wardrobe.

Channel 4 viewers wouldn't get to enjoy any of that, however. As an intern working during spring break, Mandy wouldn't show up on the air. She would ask the questions, the videographer would record the answers, and the anchorman would read the lead-in, probably written by Mandy and re-written by somebody else.

She held up a clipping of Ben Silverstein's theft story. "This kind of changes things."

No flies on you, kid. "Maybe a little," I conceded, "but I was hoping it wouldn't distract from the main story of our colloquium and the official presentation of the Woollcott Chalmers Collection."

"I'm sure you were. I'd like to talk to you on-camera about the theft and the campus police investigation."

"Fine. But first why don't you get a few minutes of Woollcott Chalmers talking? That was the original plan, and he's up next. Besides, he'll probably say something about last night's incident."

She bought it and had Smiling Sam set up his equipment at the back of the Hearth Room while Al Kane was taking questions from the audience after his talk.

When I was sure that everything was under control, I ducked down the hall and called Campus Security. I know that using a cell phone so much might cause me to have a tumor the size of an orange in my head some day, but it's an occupational hazard.

"So what have you got?" I asked Ed Decker.

"We haven't got jack."

"Would you care to elaborate?"

"Not for the press."

"Then I'll tell them you're working on it."

"That would be accurate."

I found voicemail messages left on my phone by two of the other three Cincinnati TV stations. I returned both calls quickly and confirmed the AP story. Neither pressed me for on-camera comments.

Back in the Hearth Room, the TV light was on but the camera wasn't whirling yet. Dr. Noah Queensbury was on his feet, apparently engaged in a dialogue with Kane.

". . . just as there are those who believe that Francis Bacon or a Jewish woman or someone else wrote Shakespeare's plays," he was saying. "However, the notion that Dr. Watson's literary agent, A. Conan Doyle, wrote the doctor's accounts of Sherlock Holmes should not be given credence at this colloquium."

The assertion was greeted with some laughter, but more cheers. Kane shrugged it off.

"I won't debate you, Dr. Queensbury," he said. "Let me just say that anyone who's read my novel, *The Baker Street Caper*, knows how I feel. And anyone who hasn't read it—ought to. It's on sale at the back of the room."

If it was a competition for getting laughs, Kane won. That set the stage nicely for him to clear out and let Chalmers take the lectern after a brief "man-who-needs-no-introduction" introduction from Mac.

Even though he used his cane to walk, Chalmers seemed younger, more vigorous as he stood at the front of the room. Perhaps he was even a touch defiant as he blinked his blue eyes in the glare of the TV lights.

"I'm sure you're all expecting me to say something about the theft yesterday," he said, "so I'll do that and get it over with. As you all know by now, some very valuable pieces of the Woollcott Chalmers Collection were taken. But I don't want anybody to lose sight of the fact that much more remains. The original sampling that was to be on display today is in a room sealed by the police. However, Professor McCabe and I worked with a campus librarian early this morning to put together an impromptu substitute in the rare book room of the Bennish Library. I promise you a full measure of unique and interesting items. No thief is going to spoil our weekend!"

With my brain rattling from the thunderous applause that greeted Chalmers's pronouncement, I wondered if what he and Mac had done was such a good idea. The specter of hordes of Sherlockians overrunning the rare book room by no means comforted me.

Several rows in front of where I was standing at the back of the room, Lynda leaned over to whisper to Hugh Matheson. I shifted my focus to Renata Chalmers, who was revving up the laptop set up in the middle of the room. Her husband used a remote control to click to the first PowerPoint slide. It showed a large room stuffed with books and all manner of other materials, apparently the Woollcott Chalmers Collection in its natural habitat.

"And now for a few observations on the pursuit of Sherlockiana," Chalmers said. "In four decades of collecting, I have had many disappointments, but—"

DA-da-da-da—DA-da-da! Indiana Jones. Apparently I had accidently switched my phone from vibrate to ringer mode when I returned it to my pocket. Heads turned my way from all around the room, but Chalmers talked on without a pause ("—many more triumphs") while I quickly exited through the rear door near me at the back. In the hallway I pulled out the phone to see who was calling. The little screen was filled with a photo of Darth Vader.

"Good morning, Ralph," I said. "I thought you'd call earlier."

"I only just now bought a newspaper, Cody, having waited in vain all morning for my subscription copy to show up on the lawn."

The *Observer* has a robust website for a small paper, and Lynda is pushing it strongly into social media as well with an active Facebook fan page. But apparently Ralph doesn't read the online version. The tone of his voice was accusatory, as though it were somehow my fault that he didn't get his paper. I hadn't stolen it, although that wasn't a bad idea. I made a mental note.

"Listen," Ralph went on, as if I had a choice, "you let that story get completely out of control. 'A case for Sherlock Holmes'—this is just the sort of sensationalist nonsense that I feared."

"That little thing? Probably nobody even saw it."

"You know bloody well it dominated page one! I'll be getting phone calls from the corporate sponsors about this as soon as they get off the golf course."

"Appeal to their sense of humor."

"They have none. Not when it comes to money. These are businessmen who have shareholders or partners to answer to. When they put up the funds to maintain this Chalmers Collection they didn't expect some of it to be stolen out from under us almost immediately."

"Then you should have had your curator—"

"Cody, you've got to get control of this thing. We need some positive press."

"I'm working on it. A TV4 crew from Cincinnati is taping Chalmers right now. I'm going to try to get them to stay for the presentation this afternoon, so don't forget to comb your hair."

With Father Pirelli in Rome for an important conference of his religious order, the Congregation of the Transfiguration of Our Lord, Ralph was on deck to accept the Chalmers Collection on our president's behalf at the ceremony.

"Hmmm," Ralph said, "that certainly would be helpful publicity. And I'll be sure to mention the corporate sponsors. Perhaps, Cody, you can stave off the disaster in this situation after all. You might even save your job."

Ralph's last three words were still ringing in my ear as he hung up the phone. He was happy for the moment, but I wasn't. I knew only too well that you could never count on a story going the way you hoped. Ralph's big moment could just as easily show up on the cutting room floor as on the six o'clock news. Even worse, it could be a disaster if he got caught saying the wrong thing on camera.

Chapter Nine
Smile for the Camera

"There are only three limitations to collecting Sherlockiana or anything else," Woollcott Chalmers said, leaning forward against the lectern. "They are time, space and money. The most precious of these is time. I have taken up enough of yours. Thank you for your interest."

Renata Chalmers took her huge purse off her lap and hopped up to power down the laptop. Smiling Sam waved his camera around the room to get shots of the crowd clapping.

I met Mandy Petrowski in the corridor.

"I could go on camera now if you like," I told her, "but it's going to be too noisy to do it here. Chalmers will probably be taking questions from the audience for another fifteen minutes."

But the mind inside that beautiful head of hers was going off in a different direction altogether. "How about if we get B-roll inside the room where the stuff was stolen?"

B-roll is video. I shook my head. "Sorry, no can do. It's been sealed by the police. Why don't you hang around for the ceremony where Chalmers officially presents his collection to the college? It's been moved to the library and some of the collection will be on display there."

"Well . . ." Her hair bounced like a Slinky when she cocked her head in thought.

"Our provost will be there," I prodded. "We consider this a very important event."

"We don't have time for that crap," Smiling Sam said, coming up behind me. "There's a two o'clock assignment back in Cincinnati."

So much for Ralph's TV debut.

"Then maybe I can get Mr. Chalmers to go over to the library with us as soon as he finishes here," I suggested. "He and his wife can walk you through the display. I guarantee that'll look better on the tube than the talking head of him giving his lecture. And the outside of the library would make a nice backdrop to shoot me talking about the police investigation."

"You've got all the angles covered, haven't you?" Mandy said, laughing.

"I try. Let me round up Mr. Chalmers."

I slipped back into the Hearth Room. Sebastian McCabe, his immense body scrunched into a chair to the side of the podium, saw me immediately. He stirred himself to raise one eyebrow like a question mark, then returned his attention to Hugh Matheson at the center of the room. If this was the amateur sleuth at work, Max Cutter had nothing to worry about.

Matheson was standing at his chair.

". . . taste and selection have anything to do with it, Woollcott?" he was asking. "Or are all your efforts simply focused on acquiring things that other collectors want simply because they want them?"

Chalmers forced a twisted smile onto his face and froze it there. "I only go after what I want, Hugh," he said in a surprisingly strong voice. "Trouble is, I want everything." Some chuckles responded around the room. "And as you well know, I usually get it."

"What a shame for you that getting isn't always the same as keeping," Matheson retorted.

I was glad the TV camera was no longer recording the action as Matheson sat down. The look Chalmers gave him was venomous.

The Lee J. Bennish Memorial Library is one of the oldest buildings on campus, a solid brick Georgian structure with ivy climbing up the sides. As I'd promised, it made a picturesque background for my on-camera appearance as college spokesman. Since Mandy and I had discussed the questions in advance—and I'd even suggested a few of them—there were no surprises. I described what was taken and how the loss was discovered.

"How much were the stolen items worth?" Mandy asked.

"The loss is incalculable, really, because everything taken was unique. But it's safe to say they were worth several hundred thousand dollars to a collector. The college had the entire collection insured, of course." Well, that was true, but nobody had any idea yet how much the insurer would cough up for the stolen goods, which had not been separately insured. Have you ever tried to reach *your* insurance company on a weekend?

"How did the thief get in?"

"That is still under investigation by Campus Security."

"Do they have any leads?"

"The investigation is ongoing."

After the interview we found Woollcott and Renata Chalmers already in the rare book room with our young curator, Gene Pfannenstiel. The place smelled like it had been closed up since about 1840. It was roughly the size of the Hearth Room, but felt even larger because of the thirty-foot ceiling and a balcony running around all four sides. Guards seemed to be all over the place—at least today—which eased my mind considerably about security.

Highlights from the Chalmers Collection were set up in the center of the room, many of them in glass cases—this time locked. There were foreign language editions of the Holmes canon, comic books, miniatures, artwork, statuary, dolls, and playbills.

"We had to kind of slap it together this morning," Gene apologized.

"This is incredible!" Mandy bubbled. "How can there be so much stuff about Sherlock Holmes?"

"Oh, what you see is but a small sampling of the Woollcott Chalmers Collection," Chalmers assured her. He seemed to enjoy saying the full name. "I've given forty years of my life to this."

"It *is* his life," Renata said dryly.

"Can we get on with this?" Smiling Sam said as he turned on the camera light, an unlit cigarette dangling from his lip. I think he needed a nicotine break.

Chalmers launched a guided tour of the display, showing a surprising adeptness at honing in on the materials that would play on television better than some beat-up old books.

"This playbill," he said, picking it up, "advertises the American actor William Gillette as Sherlock Holmes in the first production of his famous melodrama. It was Gillette whose preference for a curved pipe on stage fixed forever the public idea of what a Sherlock Holmes pipe looks like. That's his inscription in the corner.

"This battered tin dispatch box is just like the one where Dr. Watson kept his accounts of the adventures for which the world was not yet prepared. And these six plaster busts of Napoleon represent the central mystery in 'The Adventure of the Six Napoleons.' But this hunk of sculptured wax over here is one of my favorites."

With his cane he pointed to a colorless wax bust that was clearly supposed to be Sherlock Holmes.

"It was made by Oscar Meunier of Grenoble for Sherlock Holmes of Baker Street," Chalmers said, which was pure B.S. but I could see Mandy was eating it up. "Holmes used it to foil an assassination attempt by Colonel

Sebastian Moran in 'The Adventure of the Empty House.' Moran had planned to shoot the detective at night from across the street, using an air gun specially manufactured by the blind mechanic Von Herder. His aim at the silhouette in the window of Holmes's flat was, as you see, impeccable."

Chalmers pointed to a clean hole in the forehead of the bust.

"Awesome," Mandy said.

As Smiling Sam swept the display with his camera to give an overview of its size and scope, I noticed a particularly handsome violin in one of the display cases.

"Is that yours, Renata?" I remembered that she played the instrument professionally.

"I wouldn't dare touch it," she said with a sparkling laugh. "It's a genuine Stradivarius, probably worth more than what was stolen yesterday."

"What's it got to do with Sherlock Holmes?" Mandy asked.

"His own violin was a Strad," Chalmers explained. "He bought it from a pawn broker in Tottenham Court Road for fifty-five shillings. This one cost me considerably more."

Forty years and many thousands of dollars Chalmers had spent amassing his collection. How much it must have hurt him, I thought, to see part of it stolen. After Mandy and Smiling Sam had left, I was still thinking about how this whole business had affected Chalmers. *Maybe that was the idea*, the Max Cutter in me suggested. Maybe the whole point of the theft wasn't to possess the stolen books, or to sell them, but merely to hurt Woollcott Chalmers by stealing them.

"You don't seem to get along that well with Hugh Matheson," I told Chalmers in a careful understatement. "Do you think it's conceivable that he had anything to do with the thefts?"

Renata liked the idea, if I read the look it her dark eyes correctly, but Chalmers shot it down.

"Hugh Matheson wouldn't have the nerve or the imagination to do anything so bold," he said dismissively. "The man never dirtied his hands on anything in his life. That's why I came out the winner again and again in any competition between us to acquire some interesting piece of Sherlockiana."

"Well, then," I said, frustrated, "who knew about the display and exactly which books in it were most valuable?"

To my surprise, the gnomish Gene Pfannenstiel, who had been practically invisible as he busied himself about the display cases, blurted out, "Graham Bentley Post, I bet."

The name meant nothing to me.

"Director of the Library of Popular Culture," Gene explained. "It's a small museum and library started about ten years ago to preserve popular literary works. Post has been trying to buy the Woollcott Chalmers Collection from us ever since the word went out on the grapevine that we were getting it."

"But you can't sell my collection," Chalmers snapped. "That's one of the conditions of the gift."

"That's what I keep telling him," Gene said, "as did my predecessor before me."

Chalmers shook his white-maned head. "The fellow just won't give up, I'll grant him that. He hounded me to sell for years, but I didn't want the Woollcott Chalmers Collection to be on display up in Massachusetts with a bunch of comic books and pulp novels."

"No matter how pushy he is," I said, "I can't believe he'd come to Erin for a spot of breaking and entering."

"Maybe not," Gene said, "but he did come to Erin. He stopped by here yesterday. He said he'd be in town two or three days."

Gene scurried into a back room and returned with a business card on which Graham Bentley Post had written his hotel room number next to his cell phone number.

"I'll give him a call," I promised, pocketing the card.

Sure, it was far-fetched that a library would use crime to stock its shelves. But this was a private library, not a public one, and I didn't know how reputable it was. Besides, Post being on the scene was too much of a coincidence to just ignore. I put him on the suspect list right along with Hugh Matheson, who was still in the running in my book.

While Mac had been stuck at the colloquium, I'd flushed out two hot prospects. Max Cutter was going to solve this case, not Sherlock Holmes.

Chapter Ten
Sleuths on the Case

On my way out the front door of the Bennish
library I almost collided with the tall figure of Dr. Noah
Queensbury, who was rushing in. He excused himself
profusely.

"I don't know why you're in such a hurry," I said.
"You're already ahead of everybody else."

"My plan precisely. I intend to beat the others at
asking a few salient questions."

He struck a Sherlockian pose, which was not too
difficult considering that he was wearing a deerstalker cap.

"Others?" I repeated weakly. I was getting a grim
premonition.

"Of course! Surely I am not the only one planning
to apply the techniques of the Master to this case."

I had a sudden vision of seventy-five, eighty
Sherlockians trampling across the quadrangle, peering into
office windows, sneaking through the physical plant . . .

"Wait a minute," I said. "Don't get carried away.
This is police business. If you muck things up by sticking
your nose in, you could get yourself into some real trouble."

"The Scotland Yarders are imbeciles."

This guy just didn't know when to stop playing the
Game. He was even worse than Mac.

"The press account of this crime mentioned the
curator of rare books, one Gene Pfannenstiel," Queensbury

continued, mispronouncing the last syllable as *style* instead of *steel*. "How long has he been in this position?"

"About a month. He came highly recommended from Bowling Green State University. What the hell is that question supposed to mean?"

"Perhaps nothing at all. I am merely collecting data. 'Data! Data! Data! I can't make bricks without clay.'—'The Adventure of the Copper Beaches.' I should very much like to talk to this gentleman."

"You can talk to him all you want," I said, "but not about the crime. I'm the only source of information on that, and I can't tell you any more than you already read in the morning paper. Sorry."

"I am not quite so easily thrown off the scent, I assure you," Queensbury sniffed.

"Just remember what I said, Doc: Police business."

It was a parting shot. I took off across campus, eager to drop in on Decker and schmooze with him a little on his turf, maybe exchange some information.

Campus Security is located on the lower level of the Physical Plant. Cops and janitors, we keep 'em together. The cop shop is underground at the front, but opens to grade at the rear. Decker's office enjoys an entire wall of glass facing a greenbelt that should stay green for at least another three years until it gets paved over for parking. Decker was in.

"Don't you know it's a Saturday?" I joshed.

"What the hell," he said, "you think I work full professors' hours—two classes a week and all summer off?"

He had a printed form in one ham-like hand and a pen in another. Paperwork always makes him grumpy.

Without waiting for an invitation, I sat myself in a stuffed chair in front of Decker's Formica-topped desk. The desk is a huge thing, not elegant but practical. The framed photo on top pictured Decker's wife and four kids. The girl, Cindy, is a student at St. Benignus. There wasn't anything

else on the desk except a LIEUTENANT J. EDGAR
DECKER nameplate, a telephone, a laptop computer, a
fancy pen holder, and a piggy bank made out of a coffee can
by Decker's third-grader.

"How's Cindy doing, Ed?" I asked.

"Mostly B's."

"Good."

"Not good enough. She's smart, should be getting
straight A's. You didn't come here to talk about my
daughter's academic career, Cody."

"Well, I did hope we could discuss this Chalmers
Collection case. It's kind of politically sensitive for me
because of Ralph and the corporate sponsors and the bad
press, if you see what I mean."

Decker grunted. He didn't want to hear about
campus politics.

"So," I continued, "I was hoping you could tell me a
little more than you did on the phone."

He exhaled a bushel of air. "Means of entry still
unknown. Somebody got in and out of that room with the
goods clean as a whistle. It's weird, man."

"Anything else taken?"

He shook his head. "No.Pfannenstiel ran the
inventory for us last night and this morning. Spent hours on
it."

"How about fingerprints?"

"Pretty useless. We picked up partials from
Chalmers and his wife and Pfannenstiel, of course, and a lot
of unknowns. But hundreds of people must use that room
every week."

"So what's your best hope?"

"Off the record?"

"Sure."

"Beats me. A lot of crooks get nabbed when they try
to fence the goods, but this time . . ." He shook his head

again. I knew what he was thinking: No ordinary fence was
going to handle this kind of merchandise.

"Can't you do something visible," I said, "just so
Ralph and his friends in the business community know that
something's being done?"

"Investigations aren't supposed to be visible, Cody.
But how about this: I can send my team in to interview
everybody at this . . . "

I scotched that idea before it was even out of his
mouth. "No, thanks, Ed. There are a couple of people you
might want to keep an eye on, though." I explained about
Hugh Matheson's antagonism toward Woollcott Chalmers,
apparently exceeded only by Graham Bentley Post's lust for
the Chalmers Collection.

"Sounds pretty thin for me to do anything," Decker
said.

"I know," I admitted gloomily. "Well, I'll be seeing
these people around. I'll let you know if I come up with
anything more solid."

"Yeah, you do that."

Chapter Eleven
Power Lunching

So there I was, practically commissioned by Lieutenant Ed Decker himself to investigate this crime as well as challenged into it by Mac. And what had my brilliant brother-in-law been up to in the meantime?

Lunch.

At least, I assumed so. According to the agenda for the colloquium, chowing down had been underway for half an hour.

I did a quick-step to Muckerheide Center, to the President's Dining Room on the same floor as the Hearth Room. The luncheon crowd already had thinned out considerably from what it must have been, though, and Mac's corpulent form was nowhere in view. Off sleuthing somewhere? Doubtful. I did see Bob Nakamora heavy into conversation with a student I recognized as one of Mac's protégés, poor kid. And nearby, the woman with gray-blond hair that I recalled from last night's party sat alone, picking at a salad. Several tables away Lynda Teal was not alone. Seated obscenely close to Hugh Matheson, she seemed to hang on the lawyer's every word, a level of attention I myself had once commanded. Apparently she wanted to be his friend, too.

I went through the salad bar, picking up cottage cheese, tomatoes, onions, and peppers, while eschewing the greasy slices of pepperoni even though I love the stuff. For dessert I grabbed a banana. When I had piled my tray high with nutritious food—and made a mental note to tell Lynda about that article I read saying neurotic people live longer—I maneuvered through the sparsely populated dining room as if searching for a seat in a crowded bar. Finally I stopped at the woman sitting by herself.

"Excuse me," I said. "Mind if I sit here?"

"Not at all. I've been deserted."

Her name tag identified her as Molly Crocker from Cincinnati. Well, the Cincinnati contingent was a big one. She was in her early forties, I estimated, and took no pains to appease the Cult of Youth and Beauty. The gray streaks in her ash blond hair were untouched by dye. The hair itself had been cut in an unflattering page boy she might have done herself with a pair of scissors and no mirror. But she had a good face, handsome if not pretty. And the eyes behind her magenta glasses were lively. She was clothed in a simple print dress that bulged slightly at the tummy. Too many cookies and late night snacks or was she expecting an addition to her family? This time I remembered to check for a wedding ring—and saw one.

"Having fun?" she asked.

"Fun doesn't begin to describe it," I assured her. "I'm Jeff Cody, Sebastian McCabe's brother-in-law."

"Molly Crocker. I saw you at Mac's party, but we didn't formally meet."

"Right. Since you're from Cincinnati, what can you tell me about that dude?" I pointed discreetly at Hugh Matheson.

"Hugh? Enormously successful in his field, but you must know that. Just last week he won a damage award for six and a half million dollars based on a woman's loss of pleasure as a result of unnecessary radiation treatments to her uterus. The total award against the doctor and the radiologist, lawyer's fees included, was eight million three hundred thousand, of which Hugh took a third."

I stopped peeling my banana, impressed. "You're really up on that stuff."

She chuckled. "I ought to be."

"Opposing counsel?" I guessed.

"I was the judge in the case."

I dropped the banana. "Obviously you know a lot more about Matheson than what you read in *People* magazine."

Judge Crocker pushed away her salad, half eaten. "That's a valid deduction. What's your interest, Jeff?"

My main interest was in showing up Mac in the sleuthing department, with getting Ralph off my back a close second. But total candor was not called for in this situation.

"I'm fascinated with the collector mentality," I replied. "Chalmers spent—what, forty years?—building his collection, then today I heard that Matheson is a Holmes collector as well."

She nodded. "You've hit on a good phrase there. I know both of those men and they do share a certain 'collector mentality.' It isn't restricted to Sherlock Holmes, either, especially not with Hugh."

"What do you mean?" I looked across the room at Matheson and Lynda. He gestured with his hands, the classic motion signaling a slit throat. Lynda laughed.

"I mean," Judge Crocker said, "that he also collects women."

I took my cup of decaffeinated coffee and plunked myself down next to Lynda.

"Jeff!" said she, so startled she almost knocked her camera off the table.

"Sorry to intrude," I lied.

"Then why did you?" Lynda said. I noticed she was chewing gum, apparently a new vice acquired in the past month.

"Because I wanted to meet Mr. Matheson. Won't you introduce us?"

In a rather graceless fashion ("Jeff does PR for the local college"), she complied.

"What's your theory about the Great Sherlock Holmes Theft?" I asked.

Matheson raised his tailored eyebrows. "Do I have to have a theory?"

"Maybe not," I said, "but everybody else seems to." Actually, I hadn't talked to everybody else, but that's what came out of my mouth.

"As a matter of fact, Lynda and I were just talking about that." *I bet you were, pal.* "The obvious guess is that some collector did it or, more likely, paid to have it done. You hear about things like that with art masterpieces. Maybe what was stolen isn't worth as much as a minor Dali, but it would be priceless to a Sherlockian collector. Woollcott managed to assemble about a hundred pages of *The Hound of the Baskervilles* in Conan Doyle's own hand— more than anyone else has ever owned since the manuscript was broken up. The other *Hound* that was stolen, the first edition, was inscribed by Conan Doyle to his friend Fletcher Robinson, who inspired the story.And the *Beeton's Christmas Annual of 1887*, with the first Sherlock Holmes story, is one of only about a dozen known to exist. That alone would make it worth thousands, but this one was the presentation copy inscribed to the author's mother. That sends its value off the charts."

"You sound like you know those books almost as well as Chalmers does," I said.

"That's because Woollcott outbid me on the *Beeton's* nine years ago, screwed me out of the Fletcher Robinson *Hound*, and beat me to the punch more times than I have fingers and toes while he was scooping up all those manuscript pages."

"That nice old man?" Lynda said.

Matheson snorted. "He's done me the dirty more than a few times over the years, and every time that nice old man went further than I ever thought a person would go just to beat me out."

He rattled off a few examples—Chalmers bribing a taxi driver to get Matheson lost on the way to an important auction, Chalmers arriving at the home of a famous but impoverished Sherlockian just a few hours after his death to make the grieving widow a seemingly generous offer for his entire collection, Chalmers canceling Matheson's wake-up call at his hotel in Sussex, England, on the morning of an estate sale featuring some Conan Doyle letters.

It was a fascinating insight into the questionable methods of my college's benefactor, if true, but that wasn't getting the stolen goods back.

"Do you know a man named Graham Bentley Post?" I asked Matheson.

"I've certainly heard of him," Matheson said. He explained to Lynda about the Library of Popular Culture. "Post has a reputation for being a tiger once he goes after something."

"He's after the Chalmers Collection," I said.

"Really? But that would be for public exhibit. Stolen books wouldn't do him any good. You want to look for a private collector."

"Makes sense," I conceded, looking at the collector. "Who do you know who would be that devious and determined?"

"Only one person," Matheson said. "Woollcott Chalmers."

"Isn't there anybody else you can think of?" Lynda said. "Maybe somebody who resented Chalmers's hardball tactics?"

"If you put it that say," Matheson said with a smile, "I suppose I'd make a pretty good suspect myself."

I couldn't argue with that.

Chapter Twelve
Talking in the Library

The rare book room of the Lee J. Bennish Memorial Library looked smaller with Sebastian McCabe on the loose in there.

He dominated the place, not so much by his physical bulk—although Mac has a triple helping of that—but by the force of his energy as he moved from person to person. My brother-in-law was in his element, as buoyant as I'd ever seen him.

Finally I managed to pull him to one side.

"This morning I worked with a TV crew, almost got plowed into by Dr. Queensbury, visited Decker, talked with Judge Crocker and Matheson, and came up with a couple of good candidates for our thief," I said. "How's your day going?"

"I," declared Mac, "have been thinking."

"Now there's a stunning announcement."

"The unknown means of entry continues to interest me greatly. And I find it instructive that only a few books were taken—a handful."

"What do you think it means?"

"I am not ready to say."

"The creator of the great Damon Devlin can't do any better than that?" I jeered. "I thought you'd know whodunit by now."

Mac stroked his beard. "I could enumerate suspects aplenty, if that is what you crave. My friend Woollcott, for example, could have stolen those books out of simple avarice, though one is hard pressed to explain why he wouldnot have simply held back the books from his donation. I don't believe he is in that dire a need of a tax deduction."

"Scratch him," I agreed.

"We must turn then to other collectors, for surely it was someone of bibliographic sophistication who did this deed. The name of Hugh Matheson springs instantly to mind." He nodded toward the attorney, who was talking with Renata while Lynda took their picture. "Not for greed so much as for revenge. Even wealthy and famous individuals such as he have been known to avenge repeated slights or insults."

"Well, Matheson has suffered plenty of those, according to his own account."

Mac nodded. "If cupidity is the motive, however, the director of the Library of Popular Culture warrants a hard look."

"Graham Bentley Post?" I said.

The surprise was mutual.

"You know about him, then?" Mac said. "I do not suggest it is likely that he himself is involved. However, it is not beyond the bounds of possibility that some less scrupulous person, hearing of his late-blooming interest in Sherlockiana, looted the Chalmers Collection with the hope of peddling the materials to the Library of Popular Culture. Might I suggest an interview—"

"I'm already on it. Gene gave me Post's cell phone number and his hotel. No answer yet, but I'll get him eventually. I'll interview this dude, like any good PI would, while you're sitting on your fat rump listening to people talk about Sherlock Holmes. And I'll do it for myself, not for you."

Mac shrugged his mountainous shoulders. "Not for me the rushing to and fro of the peripatetic private investigator, Jefferson. I intend to unravel this puzzle without incurring physical exhaustion. Besides, I have other responsibilities today, one of which is to get this presentation moving now that the reprehensible Ralph has arrived."

The provost stood just inside the entrance to the rare books room, making a painful attempt to look at ease. It didn't work. There were too many sharp angles about the man, from the creases in the pants of his pinstriped suit to his nose. His slicked-back hair was shiny under the fluorescent lights.

Mac glad-handed him. "Thank you for being here to accept this important gift, Dr. Pendergast."

Ralph managed a tight smile. "Let's just get this over with, McCabe," he said, *sotto voce.*

With Ralph in tow, Mac moved to the center of the room, stealing Woollcott Chalmers away from his wife along the way. He cleared his throat, a sound not unlike the rumble of a subway train. Silence descended on cue. Without benefit of a podium, notes or microphone, my brother-in-law delivered an introduction that was part biography, part eulogy. He made it clear that Chalmers was one swell Sherlockian.

Chalmers seemed to draw strength from the applause that greeted him, as if he were feeding on it.

"Sherlock Holmes, though a natural-born actor, was not a man given to public speaking," the old man observed in a firm, loud voice, "and I always try to emulate the Master. Consequently, you can be sure this will be brief."

And it was—just three pages in the little notebook where I was recording events for an article in the alumni magazine. Having already exceeded his Biblically allotted three score and ten years, Chalmers said, it was only natural that he began to think about what would ultimately happen to the Woollcott Chalmers Collection when he had gone to that great Baker Street in the sky. At the urging of Professor

Sebastian McCabe, he had decided to donate the collection before his death to a fine institution where he could spend his final years helping to catalogue it. He knew, he said, that the collection would be in good hands. Somehow he managed to deliver that last line with a straight face, which was not only remarkable but gracious considering what had happened last night.

Ralph was equally gracious, for him.

"St. Benignus College is honored indeed to be the new home of the Woollcott Chalmers Collection," he declaimed. "This makes us number one in the Midwest as a research resource for, uh, Sherlockiana. And let me add that we are fortunate indeed to have generous outside funding, primarily from the Altiora Corporation and from the Burger Castle Company, to maintain the Collection."

He really said that, and I can prove it: I got it all on video with my iPhone, figuring I could post it later on the St. Benignus website.

Ralph then called on two dyspeptic corporate types in the crowd to take a bow for spending the shareholders' money so wisely.

Lynda stepped forward, crouched, and snapped what I figured would be a satisfying shot of Ralph, Chalmers and the corporate sponsors shaking hands all around. Ralph would love it.

That concluded the ceremony. The crowd broke up into little groups knotted around various exhibits as at a cocktail party. Matheson chatted with Gene Pfannenstiel, Judge Crocker and Dr. Queensbury huddled around the wax bust of Sherlock Holmes, and my sister and Renata listened to Al Kane hold forth.

A few people even looked at books. One of these was an older man, about six-three in height if he would stand up straight, with thick whitish-blond hair falling over one eye. Maybe I noticed him at first because he was by himself, even seeming aloof as he walked among the display cases with his hands behind his back. Or maybe it was the way he repeatedly mumbled exclamations as some title caught his attention. For whatever reason, I was already eyeing him with suspicion when he reached over as if maybe he were going to try to open the display case.

"I know what you're up to, T.J."

I whirled around and grunted at my sister, "Not exactly a secret. My job description says public relations. This is the public and I'm relating."

When I looked back the bent-over bookman was moving on to the next display.

"You know what I mean," Kate said, stepping around to get in front of me. "You're playing detective."

"Who isn't?" I grumped. "Mac insists he's going to solve this caper using his great brain, even if he doesn't leave the colloquium for the next two days. Dr. Queensbury is running around in his deerstalker cap trying to ask revealing questions. Even Al Kane has a theory. It's like they've all been infected by the Sherlock Holmes virus."

Kate absent-mindedly fingered her copper tresses. "Apparently you weren't immune from the awful contagion yourself."

"This is no game to me, Sis. There's an issue of job security, for one thing. If I can retrieve those stolen books or goose Decker into doing it, there should be enough positive media coverage in that to make even Ralph happy for a while."

The older gentleman with the hands-on approach to the Holmes display was next to Mac now, still stooped as though he were permanently bent from years of reading book titles on the lower shelves. Mac simultaneously slapped him on the arm and stole the watch off his wrist, magician-style. My brother-in-law thinks that that kind of thing is funny. What a card. Apparently the guy was a friend of Mac's. At least I hoped he was, although I hadn't noticed him at the party last night or earlier in the Hearth Room.

"I'm sure Ralph is being his usual irksome self," Kate said, "but I wonder if that's the only reason you're on this sleuthing kick?"

Thirteen lousy months—that's all that separates my sister and me in age. But she insists on being Big Sister, which includes the right to psychoanalyze me like she's Sigmunda Freud or Carla Jung or some other shrink. I wish she would stick to illustrating children's books.

"What other reasons could there possibly be?" I said, foolishly holding the door wide open for her.

"Why, to compensate for your unsuccessful attempts at mystery writing, of course—especially if you can out-sleuth Sebastian in the process. We both know it drives you crazy that his amateur detective books keep selling while your private eye novels can't find a publisher. You should try self-publishing on Kindle, by the way."

Thanks for the advice, sis. The implication of pettiness on my part stung. That was unworthy of Kate.

"You think this is some kind of ego contest between Mac and me? That's a laugh." I forced a laugh. "Besides, there isn't going to be any contest. I'm going to beat his oversized posterior."

I turned away from my sister, looking around the room for that suspicious character I'd last seen with Mac. Instead I spotted Lynda with Ralph, a truly strange duo. He was pontificating and she was getting it down in a notebook, her pen flying across the pages.

"You still look at her the same way, you know," Kate said.

"Lynda? You're imagining things. I'm just happy she asked Ralph a few questions. I'll be even happier if his deathless quotes are part of her story in tomorrow's paper."

"Don't try to tell me that lovesick expression on your face has anything to do with business. I'm an artist, remember? I've been trained to observe what I see."

"Oh, for . . . Quit trying to get into my head, will you? There's barely enough room in there for me, let alone the rest of my family."

"And it isn't just the way you look at Lynda, either," Kate persisted. "I've seen the hairy eyeball you've been giving Hugh Matheson every time he gets close to her. If looks could kill . . ."

"Sure, I've been watching him," I acknowledged. "Matheson happens to be a choice suspect in this little caper, that's all."

Kate just looked at me. That woman could stare down Svengali.

"Okay, okay," I said. "How am I supposed to feel when I see a woman I used to be pretty close to chumming it up with a guy like that? I've read all those stories about Matheson's three ex-wives and too many bimbos to count. He may be rich and famous and handsome, but I don't think he'd be any good for her."

"There you go again, T.J., deciding what's good for Lynda. You know she—"

"I know she's through with me for good. Oh, except that she wants to be friends. Don't forget that part." Did I sound bitter?

I moved to leave on that exit line, but Kate tugged on my shoulder. "She still looks at you the same way, too, T.J. And not like a friend."

Session Two

2:00   "Nick Carter, Alias Sherlock Holmes"—
        Professor Malcolm Whippet, Licking Falls
        State College

2:30   "Sherlock Holmes in Scandinavia"—Lars
        Jenson, Lund, Sweden

3:00   "Holmes and Drugs: Was Sherlock's Coke
        the Real Thing?"—Dr. Noah Queensbury,
        BSI, Cincinnati

3:30   Interval: Field Bazaar

4:00   "Disguise in the Canon"—Barry Landers,
        St. Benignus College

4:30   "And Ladies of the Canon"—KathleenCody
        McCabe, Erin, Ohio

Chapter Thirteen
I Can't Believe This

Listening to Professor Malcolm Whippet of Licking Falls State College, the first speaker of the afternoon session, was like suffering a Chinese water torture of words.

Whippet was a frail figure in his late sixties, medium height, thin, with a high forehead, fringes of gray hair, age spots on his head and hands, and gray-green eyes. He was so slight he hardly seemed to be there at all.

Whenever he had to turn the pages of the paper he was reading, he stopped his nasal monotone to lick his fingers. After a few introductory comments ("Let us begin with the obvious—Sherlock Holmes was an American"), Professor Whippet's presentation on "Nick Carter, Alias Sherlock Holmes" turned out to be a pastiche, an imitation Holmes story. Whippet lacked, however, a few tools of the storyteller's art, such as a sense of pace, an ear for dialogue, and a rudimentary notion of plot. Also, he couldn't write.

"'Yes, my faithful Watson, it is quite so!'" he read. "'All these years I have concealed my true identity even from you. I am indeed Nicholas Carter, the famous American detective!'"

Putting a hand over my mouth to stifle an impolite sound, I looked around the room to see how this was going over with the Sherlockian set. A lot of people were shifting in their seats, including Lynda and Matheson. They were still sitting next to each other and Lynda wasn't sending any lovesick looks *my* way, contrary to my sister's observation.

Mac had deposited himself in a wingback chair next to me at the back of the room. I leaned over to tell him, "I can't believe this. How do this guy's students stand it?"

"Students?" Mac repeated with dismay. He raised an eyebrow. "Surely you jest. Professor Whippet has tenure, not students. Do not demean the man's achievements, Jefferson. It takes considerable talent to make Sherlock Holmes this boring. I had no idea he had it in him."

Whippet droned on. I looked at my watch: two-eleven. When it seemed like half an hour had passed, I looked at it again: two-fourteen. Would it never end? It did, finally, but not until the speaker had run five minutes over his allotted time and brought into his story Mycroft Holmes (revealed as one of Nick Carter's operatives), Grover Cleveland, Fu-Manchu, Jack the Ripper, Count Dracula, Oscar Wilde, the Prince of Wales, and Tinker Bell.

When the concluding cliché had been uttered, the applause of a grateful crowd shook the room. Nobody called for more.

Next up on the program was a man Mac introduced to my surprise as Lars Jenson, the most prominent Swedish publisher of the Sherlock Holmes stories. I'd known he was coming, of course—from a conference in New York, not directly from Sweden. But I had never connected his name with the stoop-shouldered fellow from the rare book room, the one with the whitish-blond hair hanging over one eye à la Carl Sandburg. Dressed in a double-breasted blue suit, pink shirt, wide paisley tie, and socks with little clock designs on them, he didn't look like my idea of a publisher.

When he opened his mouth, Jenson sounded like the Swedish Chef on *The Muppet Show*. Approximately every other word started with either a "y" or a "v" sound, which made it hard to figure out what he was saying. There was something about Sherlock Holmes helping the King of Scandinavia on two occasions, and Holmes and Watson visiting Norway at the end of one of their adventures. And

Holmes, if I caught it right, once adopted the guise of a Norwegian explorer. But don't expect me to give you quotes.

All the while he talked, Jenson kept playing with a pair of horn-rimmed glasses. He'd put them on, yank them off, put them on, yank them off. There seemed no rhyme or reason to it, since he didn't use the glasses to read from notes. For awhile I was fascinated, trying to figure out a pattern. But it started giving me the heebie-jeebies until finally I couldn't stand it anymore and I left.

Out in the corridor, haunted by that Swedish Chef voice coming over the loudspeaker, I flipped out my iPhone. After posting a quick tweet (*"Last two speakers at Doyle-Holmes colloquium truly unbelievable"*), I called a certain cell phone number. Graham Bentley Post answered with his names—all three of them—on the third ring.

"This is Thomas Jefferson Cody," I informed him, not to be outdone in the multiple names department. "I'm calling from St. Benignus College and I'd like to talk to you about the Woollcott Chalmers Collection."

"Indeed?" His voice turned warmer, say three degrees. "I have already had some discussions of that nature with Mr. Pfannenstiel. They have not been fruitful."

"I know," I said. "When and where can we meet?"

He suggested six-thirty and dinner at the restaurant in the Winfield, which is top-notch, but I planned to stick with the colloquium right through the seven o'clock banquet in the President's Dining Room. Post had an appointment at a private home on Everly Street until after five o'clock, so we agreed to meet at five-thirty at the nearby main branch of the Sussex County Public Library.

"I hope you'll have some news for me, Mr. Cody," Post said.

"That goes double," I assured him.

As I disconnected, I wondered why Post hadn't even mentioned the theft last night. It seemed a remarkable oversight—unless he'd been deliberately avoiding the subject.

My spot on the couch at the back of the Hearth Room had been swiped by a man in a string tie, so I slipped into a chair in the last row. I was in front of Mac and lined up almost exactly behind Lynda and Matheson, who leaned over to whisper things to her with alarming frequency—alarming to me, anyway.

Dr. Queensbury had the lectern, discussing Sherlock Holmes and cocaine. Still wearing the deerstalker cap, he paced and postured like the great detective himself as he quoted alternatively from the Holmes stories and from the British medical journals of the day. I wrote down some of his more memorable points:

"Watson mentions Holmes's use of cocaine only five times, and all of them in stories appearing between 1890 and 1893."

"In 1890 cocaine was still considered a therapeutic agent. It was a non-prescription drug. Not until the middle of the decade did Freud reject it.

"It has been questioned, however, whether Holmes really used cocaine at all. Perhaps he was just having Watson on."

Queensbury's talk had at least one outstanding virtue: It was only about fifteen minutes long. Even after he took questions from the floor the program was running ahead of schedule. Queensbury sat down, amid applause, and there was an awkward gap when he wasn't replaced at the lectern. I looked behind me but the master of ceremonies, Mac, was no longer there either. Finally, my sister Kate stood up and announced that it was time for an "interval" or break between sessions.

The flow of the crowd went in two directions—either out the doors (heading for such amenities as coffee, the restroom, or a place to smoke outside) or toward the back of the room, where the bald man was selling books and what I would call trinkets.

As I stood up to stretch my longish legs, I heard somebody behind me at the book table say:

"I have that book!"

"British or American edition?" another voice asked.

"Both."

Stirring stuff, but where in the world was Mac? I wanted to tell him about my appointment with Graham Bentley Post. Queensbury's talk coming up short obviously had caught Mac off guard. Looking around the room I still didn't see his huge form.

"Jeff!"

I sure liked that voice. Renata Chalmers, flashing that thousand-watt smile at me, nudged her way through some of the reveling Sherlockians until she stood at my side. She pushed a wild strand of black hair out of her eye and stuck her hands into the pockets of her dress-for-success suit.

"What do you hear from the campus police?"

"Nothing worth repeating."

"No theories at all?"

"Oh, there are theories galore," I said, lowering my voice, "but not from the cops."

"Really?" Oh, that smile. "Please tell me. I just love theories."

I shook my head. "No way am I going to name names. I could be slandering somebody."

And considering who one of my hot suspects was, a legal battle was the last thing I wanted.

I could have sworn Renata was about to resort to feminine wiles—something about the man-eating look in her brown eyes as she opened her mouth—but just then her husband limped by and she buttoned up.

"Hello, Cody," he said, giving me one of the man-to-man slaps on the arm that I've always hated. "The program seems to be going well despite last night's unfortunate curtain-raiser."

He leaned on his cane and we exchanged pleasantries. I told Chalmers how much I enjoyed his morning talk. He said he was quite pleased with the way the Chalmers Collection looked in our library. I assured him that Campus Security was doing everything possible to recover the rest of the collection. After a minute or two of that, the Chalmerses left to powder their noses or whatever and I was left pondering the books for sale. Some were old and possibly rare, while others were new or even paperback. How could there be so much written about one thin guy with abominable taste in headgear?

The bald bookseller smiled, showing a gold tooth, and pointed to one slim volume with a garish cover. "There's a new one," he said helpfully.

I picked up the book and checked out the title: *The Adventure of the Unique 'Hamlet.'*

"It's actually an old story, of course, the famous Vincent Starrett pastiche, but a new edition with some cool illustrations," the dealer said. "You've probably read it."

"I'm afraid not."

"Well, it's about a bibliophile who asks Holmes to solve the theft of his rare edition of *Hamlet.*"

"How timely," I said dryly.

The bookman nodded. "In this story the client did it himself—to hide the fact that the supposedly rare volume was a fake."

From behind me a familiar voice said: "An excellent volume you have there, Jefferson! It was one of the early pastiches, and it remains one of the finest."

I whirled on my brother-in-law. "I set up an interview with Post. Where the hell have you been?"

"I the hell have been conversing with Lieutenant Decker, asking him the key questions that will solve this elementary case."

"Oh, yeah? Such as?"

He shook his hairy head. "On that point I remain coy, Jefferson. Perhaps my little idea is all wrong and you would think less of me later."

"You? Wrong?" I forced out what I hoped was an obviously faked chuckle.

"Yes, the notion is risible, is it not?" Mac gestured with the unlit cigar in his hand. "Let us say, then, that I will not answer that question because no good amateur sleuth would—not Ellery Queen, not Amelia Peabody, not Damon—"

"Oh, just stuff it, Mac. You can't hand me that crap."

"I just did, old boy."

The lights in the Hearth Room flicked off, on, off, on. Somebody was trying to tell us something.

"Not another word, Jefferson," Mac said. "We shall have to recommence this verbal ballet later. The interval is over."

Chapter Fourteen
Master of Disguise

Barry Landers was a student of Mac's, which put his most likely age between eighteen and twenty-one. Wearing jeans and a yellow and black Sherlock Holmes T-shirt as he stood at the lectern, he looked even younger. He was short, overweight, baby-faced.

But he talked with confidence and authority, using a vocabulary that was closer to Sebastian McCabe than something he might have picked up from watching teen-oriented television.

"Sherlock Holmes is, to use an overused phrase, a 'master of disguise,' " he said. "We're not only told this in the canon, we're shown it. At different times Holmes appears as a common loafer, a drunken groom, the Irish-American Altamont, the rakish young plumber Escott, a French workman, an Italian priest, a Non-conformist clergyman, Captain Basil, an opium smoker, the explorer Sigerson, an elderly bookseller, and an old woman."

Disguise, yet. And Mac sat there, back at the front of the room now, hanging on every word as if he could disguise himself as, say, a "rakish young plumber." Was he really on to something with whatever he had asked Decker or was it just B.S.? A toss-up. With Mac you could never tell. He was, after all, a professor.

"What is interesting to note," Barry Landers went on as I inched my way toward the door, "is that Holmes himself is more than once fooled by disguise. In *A Study in*

Scarlet, Jefferson Hope's friend poses as an older woman, causing Holmes to say later, 'We were old women to be taken in.' And in another famous sex reversal, Irene Adler dresses as a man the evening she walks by Holmes in Baker Street and says, 'Good-night, Mr. Sherlock Holmes.' "

By this time I was in the corridor, pulling out my phone. I called Decker.

"You again?" he grumped.

"Show some gratitude. I saved your butt from a TV crew today, now I hear you're talking about the crime to Mac."

"He caught me by surprise." Decker did not sound pleased.

"What did he ask you?"

"A bunch of stuff about keys to the room where the books were stolen," Decker said. "Things like, 'How many are there?' and 'Who has them?' Pretty basic."

"So what did you tell him?"

"Running down the keys wasn't exactly brain surgery," Decker said. "We did that before I went to bed this morning. Call it five keys altogether, counting the masters that open every door in Muckerheide. Nick Caruso and Bobby Deere each have masters they carry all the time." Caruso runs the Center by day; Deere sleeps there at night. "Campus Security has another master that's picked up by the guard at the beginning of his shift. The Muckerheide Center office has two individual keys to Hearth Room C. One was safely locked away there last night; Deere showed it to us. The other was on loan to Gene Pfannenstiel, who recklessly gave it out—"

"—to Sebastian McCabe," I finished. "So every key is accounted for?"

"Tighter than a drum. Pfannenstiel swears up and down he never had his key out of his hands until he slipped it to McCabe around seven last night. And the one that was still in the Center office hadn't been signed out all day."

"And what did Mac say to that?"

"He wanted to know if it was shiny. I told him I didn't know."

"Shiny? What's that supposed to mean?" I demanded.

"Damned if I know. He's your brother-in-law."

"Don't rub it in. Did he say anything else?"

"Yeah. He said I should find out, and that the key he used last night—the one I made him turn in to me—*wasn't* shiny."

Chapter Fifteen
"Women Are Never to Be Trusted"

I was supposed to meet Graham Bentley Post at five-thirty. Eager as I was to be on with it, my watch told me that was still forty-five minutes away. I returned to the Hearth Room, standing just inside the door at the front where, for a change, I could scan the faces of the crowd instead of bad haircuts.

My sister was at the lectern.

". . . and Holmes himself repeatedly misstates his own posture toward the female of the species. In *The Sign of Four*, for example, he says that 'love is an emotional thing, and whatever is emotional is opposed to that true cold reason which I place above all things. I should never marry myself lest I bias my judgment.' Holmes implies here a calculated neutrality with regard to women. This is patently false. Elsewhere in the same book Holmes tells the good Watson, 'women are never to be trusted—not the best of them.' That is hardly a neutral attitude."

Hugh Matheson slid his arm across the back of Lynda's chair as he leaned forward to whisper some sweet nothing. Pained, I looked around the room, making a little game out of seeing how many faces I recognized. There were quite a few: Kane, Queensbury, Crocker, Nakamora, the ineffable Professor Whippet . . .

"And in 'A Scandal in Bohemia,' " Kate continued, "Watson reports that Holmes 'never spoke of the softer passions, save with a gibe and a sneer.' Does that sound like a man purged of all emotions toward the opposite sex? On the contrary, Holmes displays quite a strong emotion—a negative one. Was he, then, a born misogynist as some would have us believe—or even a homosexual? I submit that the opposite is true. At some point in his unrecorded past Sherlock Holmes loved well but not wisely. He was, in short, 'burned.'"

Now *there* was something I could relate to, I thought bitterly.

Kate went on to talk about Irene Adler (*"the* woman"), Mary Sutherland, Violet Hunter, and other strong females in the canon. She attributed their dynamic portrayals to the influence of Arthur Conan Doyle's own strong-willed mother. Dr. Queensbury was just rising, apparently to object to this gratuitous reference to Conan Doyle, when I checked my watch again and saw that nearly half an hour had flown by and Kate's talk was running over. If I didn't make tracks I'd keep the man from the Library of Popular Culture waiting.

My brother-in-law, sitting near the lectern just across from where I was standing, seemed too engaged in the looming confrontation between his wife and Queensbury to notice my departure. In the corridor I thought I had gotten away clean until one of the voices I know best called after me. "Jeff!"

Lynda Teal.

I retracted my foot from the down escalator, almost slipping in the process.

For once Lynda looked slightly less than perfect, even to me. One or two strands of honey-colored hair were out of place and her blouse was disheveled. She was chewing gum. Still, I found myself having to fight off thoughts of a romantic and even biological nature.

"Where are you sneaking off to?" she demanded.

"The men's room," I said, the first thing that came into my head.

"Baloney. You don't have to go downstairs for a john. Look, I saw you and Mac conniving during the last break. You two are up to something and I want to know what it is. It's something about those stolen books, right?"

"So it's not my rugged good looks or my charming personality that has you so interested in my activities all of a sudden. You're just chasing a story."

"Well, yeah. It's what I do." She leaned against the escalator. "I'm a journalist." *As if I needed reminding.*

I shook my head sadly. "And to think we used to have such good times together."

"Didn't we, Jeff? And always I'll remember. Now, what's Mac got you doing this time?"

I snorted. "This is my game plan, not Mac's."

"Okay. What is it, then—a clue, a witness, a suspect?"

"Something like that. I'm supposed to meet a guy in—" I looked at my watch. "Damn. Ten minutes. I'll never make it."

"I'll give you a ride. My car'll get you wherever you're going a lot faster than that bicycle of yours. You *are* still riding the bike everywhere you don't walk, aren't you?"

"Not everywhere. I still have the Beetle for trips over ten miles." Even to me that sounded lame. I hurried on. "This is a solo venture, Lynda. Besides, you wouldn't want to leave the great Hugh Matheson all alone, would you?"

"He's got his ego to keep him company."

"You didn't seem to mind while you were sitting with him all day."

"I was being polite."

"Polite? He was whispering in your ear!"

"Yeah, mostly about his favorite subject—him."

"This has been great, Lynda, but I really—"

"You have less time now than you did five minutes ago. How about that ride?"

The doors of the Hearth Room sprang open and people started pouring out. Matheson was near the head of the herd, busy bending Judge Crocker's ear.

"Okay, okay," I said, making the snap decision that put me right in the thick of the mess that followed. "Let's just get out of here."

We ran down the escalator to the main level of Muckerheide Center and out a side door to the campus street where Lynda's yellow Mustang was illegally parked.

As soon as I got into the car, I noticed something different.

"Hey, it doesn't smell like an ashtray anymore," I said.

"I gave up smoking and took up running," Lynda explained as she set her camera and purse on the floor behind the driver's seat.

I stared at her. She studiously ignored me.

"That's great," I said finally. "Good for you. Why didn't you do that all those years I was nagging you to?"

"Because you were nagging me to. Now, who is this guy you're supposed to meet?"

While she drove the car and chewed a fresh stick of gum, I filled her in on Graham Bentley Post and his obsession to possess the Woollcott Chalmers Collection for his museum. By the time we reached the Sussex County Library, she knew as much about Post as I did.

The main branch happens to be on Mulberry Street, not Main. It's an Andrew Carnegie library, a brick and stone structure built more than a hundred years ago and seemingly good for at least a hundred more.

From several blocks away I spotted the man pacing in front of the broad front steps. He was in his early fifties, medium height and build, with thick black hair, a gray mustache, and the chiseled features of a comic book superhero. Lynda parked in front of the fire hydrant and I hopped out.

"Thanks for the ride," I told Lynda.

"Oh, no, you don't. I'm not just your damned chauffeur."

She got out of the car and scrambled after me. There was nothing I could do without creating a scene in front of Graham Bentley Post, assuming it was he.

"Mr. Post?" I said, approaching him with an extended hand. "I'm Thomas Jefferson Cody."

Post was wearing a tailored blue suit without a single loose threat. He glanced at the slightly battered Mustang and then at me as if he doubted my statement, but he shook my hand anyway. I introduced Lynda as my associate.

"Partner," she said firmly. *Hey, I like the sound of that! Too bad you don't really mean it; not the way I'd like.*

Post skipped the small talk. "You are late, Mr. Cody. I can only trust that your arrival will prove worth waiting for. Let me be succinct: What kind of a deal can we cut that will put the Chalmers Collection into my hands?"

"We're not—" Lynda began.

"We're not sure what you have in mind," I interrupted. "The college can never sell the Collection, of course. It was a gift."

"Perhaps not," Post conceded, fingering his mustache, "but with the right inducement—perhaps the promise of naming a small edifice on campus in his honor—Mr. Chalmers might be persuaded to withdraw his gift and sell it to the Library of Popular Culture at a handsome price."

"And what would be in that for the college?" I asked.

"I believe I could arrange for another collection to be donated to St. Benignus, one with greater prestige and monetary value but of less interest to my institution."

"Quite a scenario," I said. "Machiavelli would be green with envy. You should bounce the idea off of our provost."

Post looked at me as if he had smelled something bad and I was it. "You have no authority to negotiate?"

"None."

"Then you have wasted my time. We have nothing to discuss." He started to walk away.

"I was hoping you could tell me—us—a little about the market for those parts of the collection that were stolen last night," I called after him.

That stopped him cold. "Stolen? What the devil are you talking about?"

"Didn't you read about it in the local paper this morning?" Lynda asked.

"I only read the *New York Times* and I find it appalling that I was unable to purchase a copy at my hotel this morning."

While Lynda looked daggers at the blowhard, fuming silently, I told Post what had been taken.

"Virtually priceless," Post gasped. "Of course they have a very high monetary value, hundreds of thousands of dollars or more, but that is quite beside the point. Those are one-of-a-kind items—and stolen right out from under your nose. I assure you nothing like that could ever happen at the Library of Popular Culture!"

"I bet you can't wait to give Chalmers the same assurance," Lynda said. "You'd probably even pay for some legal talent to help him withdraw his donation. Then he could give the collection to an institution where it would be safe—yours, for example."

"That is . . . preposterous," Post sputtered. "It would be highly unethical for us to take advantage of this unfortunate situation."

Lynda snorted. "That's not the worst thing you might be suspected of before this is all over."

Post's jaw obeyed the law of gravity. He fixed Lynda with eyes of ice. "Are you daring to imply that I might be connected in any way with this criminal activity?"

"She's saying some people might think so," I interpreted, trying to unruffled his feathers a bit. "It's awfully convenient that you just happened to be in Erin the day that stuff was stolen."

"I have a perfectly good reason for being in this insufferable little burg," Post said.

After an awkward pause, I prodded him: "Care to tell us what it is?"

"No, I would not! It's a highly confidential matter, as many of our acquisitions are."

"I can appreciate that," I said with what I hoped was a gracious nod. "But I'm sort of working with Campus Security in this matter, and I'm sure it would help them to rule you out of any possible involvement if you'd reveal why you're in town."

"No."

"I'm just afraid that if Campus Security calls you in for an interview the press might get wind of it," I said. I was playing good cop/bad cop against the hypothetical media. "You know how they are," Lynda chimed in.

"Oh, all right, then," Post snapped. "But only if you agree to keep this strictly confidential." We agreed, although I could read the reluctance in Lynda's eyes as if it were a newspaper headline. She was agreeing to go off the record without the slightest idea of what she was going to hear. "I am in Erin negotiating with a man named Jaspers to acquire the largest privately held collection of Harvey Comics, some issues going back to the beginnings of the company in 1940."

The smug look on his face told me this was something special, but I didn't get it. I mean, everybody knows Superman. Spider-Man and Batman I'd read as a kid. X-MenI was familiar with from the movies. But who was Harvey, other than an invisible bunny in an old movie?

"Harvey Comics is Casper the Friendly Ghost," Post explained, "as well as Richie Rich, Baby Huey, Little Audrey—virtually a treasure house of popular culture."

It was the mission of the Library of Popular Culture to acquire popular forms of literature for public display and for the use of scholars, Post explained. In pursuit of that mission he'd been trying for years to convince Alfred Jaspers, Sr., to sell his Harvey Comics collection, but without success. Jaspers had died last fall, however, and his son was willing to cash out. The younger Jaspers had invited Post to Erin to discuss the price on Friday. The bargaining was hard and carried over to today, when a deal was struck.

The story seemed plausible and checkable. Post did have a good reason for being in Erin other than the presence of the Chalmers Collection. He readily admitted, however, that he had visited Gene Pfannenstiel on Friday—unaware that the young man had no bargaining authority—before keeping his appointment with Jaspers.

"We have tens of thousands of comics at the Library of Popular Culture, but little Sherlockiana," Post said. "It would be a tremendous coup to fill that gap by acquiring one of the largest and most prestigious Sherlock Holmes collections in private hands."

"What you're saying is, you were hungry," Lynda pointed out. "So hungry you weren't going to give up even after Chalmers had decided on his donation to the college. Who knew that?"

Post shrugged. "Assorted bibliophiles, I suppose. Word gets around. Why?"

"Because no ordinary thief took that stuff in hopes of fencing it," I said, catching her reasoning right away. "It was either a Sherlockian who wanted to gloat over the books in private or somebody who knew where the market was for things like that. And it looks like you're the market."

Post drew himself up in a dignified posture reminiscent of the ramrod-straight Woollcott Chalmers. "I am not a receiver of stolen goods, Mr. Cody!"

"Of course not," I agreed, visions of a slander suit dancing in my head. "But please get in touch with me or with Lieutenant Decker of our Campus Security if you even suspect that someone is trying approach you with those books." I gave him my card.

"You may be certain that I will do so," Post said stiffly, without a glance at the card.

He carried his injured dignity away in a late model BMW, midnight blue.

"What do you think?" I asked as he drove off.

Lynda shook her honey-colored curls all over the place. "No way he's the thief—he'd be too afraid of getting lint on his suit. And stolen goods would be no good to his library-cum-museum anyway because they couldn't be displayed or made available to scholars. A professional thief would know that, so the idea that somebody took the stuff to sell to Post doesn't wash, either."

We climbed into the Mustang. It was six o'clock and we'd spent nearly half an hour going nowhere with Post.

A collector as thief still made the most sense— somebody like Hugh Matheson, Lynda's newfound friend. But I didn't say that. I didn't say much at all until Lynda pulled the Mustang behind Muckerheide Center, right where my bike was parked. She left the motor running.

"You aren't staying for the banquet?" I asked, my hand on the door. Maybe that was wishful thinking— because if she were coming to the banquet, she probably wouldn't be sitting alone.

"I'm coming back for it," Lynda said, adjusting the rear-view mirror. "First I'm going home to play with my hair a little, change my clothes."

"You look fine to me."

"Thank you, but Victorian dress is optional and I plan to take the option."

"You could wear that frilly thing you had on at that Halloween party two years ago. Remember the moon and the music and—"

"Jeff," she cut in, "the cocktail hour begins in half an hour. I'd better go."

I sighed. "It's been good to be around you again. Whatever happened to us, Lynda?"

"You smothered me, Jeff, that's all. You were domineering and bossy and every other word that describes a man who wanted to run my life like it was his own. I wasn't born to be a trained pet. And did I ever tell you that you're also jealous and stubborn?"

"Frequently." *Maybe I shouldn't have asked that question.* "But come on, now, you like me anyway, don't you—at least a little?" I was trying to keep the mood light because I didn't want to leave her on down note.

"Like you? God help me, Jeff Cody, I still love you, you idiot. Now please get out of my car."

I couldn't begin to understand that, much less think of an exit line, so I just closed the car door and headed for Muckerheide. After just a few steps in that direction I looked back to follow Lynda with my eyes. The Mustang was getting ready to turn left out of the parking lot.

Left, I realized with a start. That wasn't the way to Lynda's apartment.I followed her so fast I didn't even put on my bicycle helmet.

And that's how I wound up in a hallway at the Winfield Hotel, with Lynda in my arms talking about murder.

Chapter Sixteen
"We'll Know It When We See It"

I hugged her for while, then pulled away and pounded on the door. Lynda shook her head. "No use knocking. He won't hear you."

"Get me in there."

She pulled a flat rectangular key card out of her purse, slid it into the opening, got the green light, and pushed open the door. I brushed past her into a luxurious Winfield room with real paintings on the walls and heavy quilt spreads on the two beds.

Hugh Mathesonlay on his back on the floor a few feet from the first bed. Bright red blood had gushed out of the right side of his neck, dripping on the deep pile carpet. The lawyer's blue eyes, fixed and unseeing, stared up at the ceiling.

It seemed impossible that a spark of life could remain in the motionless body. But if there was even the slightest chance . . .

I moved toward Matheson.

"The place in the neck where you check for a pulse isn't even there anymore," Lynda said. "He's dead, all right. And he didn't do it to himself. I could see right away that there's no gun nearby." Her voice was jagged, bordering on hysteria.

"He was shot? How could you even tell with all that blood?"

"I looked closely. I've seen autopsy pictures."

She looked away from the body and hugged her shoulders as if trying to warm up in a deep freeze. She breathed in deep gasps. I was feeling sick and scared myself, but I had to keep it together for her sake. Lynda may be the toughest person I know, but right now she needed a rock to hold on to.

"It's going to be okay," I promised, wrapping a comforting arm around her. "I'll get you out of this somehow. I know you didn't do it. You didn't have the time."

She jerked away from me. "Didn't have the—That's how you know I didn't kill him? Of course I didn't kill him. Who the hell would think that I killed him?"

"Almost anybody but me who found you leaving a hotel room with a fresh body in it," I said. My voice rose a bit. "And I do mean fresh. The blood is still wet."

Lynda glanced at the gruesome thing on the floor, then looked away again. I couldn't blame her, but I felt guilty for being so repulsed at the bloody sight. He had, after all, been a human being.

"I was leaving to get the manager so he could call the police," Lynda said. "What are you doing here, anyway?"

"I followed you from Muckerheide on my bike."

"What! I can't believe it. No, wait. You're Jeff Cody. I believe it." *Was that irony or sarcasm, Lynda? I still get the two confused.* "What a sneaky thing to do."

"*I* was sneaky? You're the one who lied about where you were going. But I can see why you didn't want to tell me you were coming here to meet Matheson in his room."

"So that's what you think! I should have known. Damned jealous . . . You've got the wrong idea totally. Matheson came on to me—"

"Then I don't have the wrong idea," I interrupted.

"Shut up. Sitting next to me at the colloquium he kept on and on about his collection of Sherlockiana andmade snide comments about Chalmers's. He didn't even try to hide his delight that somebody had made off with the best parts. I figured it was probably Matheson who'd done it, or somebody paid by him, and that he would brag about the whole thing if I got him loosened up enough."

"Hence the key, I suppose—part of the loosening up process."

Lynda nodded. "When he invited me to have a few drinks with him, I suggested we go someplace where we could talk quietly. I'm sure he didn't think I really meant talk, but I did. Anyway, Matheson said he was going to try to have a word with somebody for a few minutes right after Kate's talk. He slipped me a key to this room and told me to wait for him if he didn't show up right away. I was hoping to beat him here and look around for the stolen books, but talking to Post ran a little long and I was too late for that."

"Matheson didn't say who he was meeting?"

"No."

"Of course not. That would be too easy. All right, try this on for size: Suppose the meeting turned nasty and they parted with words. The other person could have come here later with a gun and plugged Matheson."

Lynda grimaced. "We'd better let the police deal with that."

"The police?" If I sounded incredulous, it's only because I was. "Don't you know what Oscar would do if his people were to find you with that?" I pointed to the late Hugh Matheson, his life's blood seeping into the expensive carpet of the Winfield Hotel.

"Muck up the evidence?" Lynda said.

"Hang you out to dry, that's what. He's been looking for an excuse for months. A murder charge is beyond his wildest dreams."

Oscar Hummel is Erin's chief of police, a retired desk sergeant from Dayton who never tires of telling Mac how unrealistic his Damon Devlin plots are. (I'll give him points for that.) He'd had a feud going with Lynda over unfavorable coverage of his department in her paper. Last winter one of his overeager officers had arrested an out-of-town drug dealer who turned out to be under surveillance by the Sussex County Sheriff's Department. The evidence was thrown out of court for lack of a search warrant and the dealer walked. Then earlier in the spring, Oscar himself—in hot pursuit of a stolen truck—had driven his cruiser through a cornfield. *The Erin Observer & News Ledger's* editorial asserted that the chief's operation had gone "from Keystone Kops to bull in a china shop." As news editor, Lynda didn't write the editorials, but that distinction was lost on Oscar.

"That's absurd," Lynda said. "What possible reason would I have—"

"Lovers' quarrel."

She said a rude word, followed by, "I barely knew the man. And what would you be doing here—cheering me on?"

Apparently the question was hypothetical, because she didn't wait for an answer before she reached into the outside pocket of her purse and pulled out her Android.

"No you don't," I said firmly, grabbing the phone. "If you don't believe that scenario will appeal to Oscar, how do you think he'd like the ever-popular 'Love Triangle with Jealous Ex-Boyfriend'? Consider what we have here: you, me, and a formerly handsome corpse. Oscar may not be as dumb as he likes to pretend sometimes, but he is totally lacking in imagination. He always goes for the most obvious explanation. Remember the Parsons case?"

When a popular city councilman was strangled with his own necktie, Oscar arrested his promiscuous wife. But her attorney proved in court that Parsons had died during an autoerotic evening gone awry.

"But Oscar's your buddy," Lynda objected.

"I'd say we're friendly in a casual way. He calls me once in a while when he gets free tickets to a Reds or Bengals game, and I've gone fishing with him a few times when I had questions about police procedure for a mystery I was working on. But I don't think our personal relationship would hold him back for twelve seconds from doing his job if he thought I'd killed a man, not even if we were best pals."

"So that's what you're really afraid of!"

"Partly," I conceded, hoping to disarm her with my candor. Actually, it was a tossup between Oscar's jail and Ralph's wrath as to which I was more afraid of. Ralph would not like for me to have found a body. "But I'm worried about you, too."

Spearing me with a skeptical look, Lynda yanked her phone back, but returned it to her purse.

"Well, we can't just leave the body here to rot."

"We'll call the police from the pay phone."

There was still one left in Erin, about two blocks from the Winfield.

"All right, all right," Lynda said. "Whatever you say. Let's just get the hell out of here."

I shook my head. "We can't just leave. We have to search the room first."

"For what?"

"For any clues that Oscar and his crew might not understand," I said. "Something Sherlockian maybe."

"If you have some crazy idea of solving the murder, forget it. That's police business."

"Tell that to Mrs. Parsons."

"Let's leave, Jeff. Please."

"You can go."

"I don't want to be alone." She pulled a stick of gum out of her purse.

"Don't leave the wrapper here," I warned her. "When did you start chewing gum, anyway?"

"When I gave up smoking," she said. "I eat too much candy, too, and pretty soon I'm going to get fat. Quit giving orders. And make this fast, will you?"

This was no time to tell her that she'd probably be okay on the weight because of the running. I got down on my knees in front of the bed closest to the door and flipped up the bedspread. "It would go faster if you'd help," I said.

"Then I'll help."

Good girl, I thought but did not say.

A minute went by while I crawled as far under the bed as I could.

"Nothing under here," Lynda reported from beneath the other bed. "Not even dust bunnies."

"Same here," I said.

Standing up, I stepped around the hideous corpse and looked at the night stand. Bingo. Right next to the hotel phone was a notepad with the fancy Winfield Hotel logo on top. The number 525 was neatly written on it in blue ink. I copied the number into the reporter's notebook I carry in my back pocket.

"What's that?" Lynda asked from the other side of the bed.

"Probably a hotel room number that Matheson called. Maybe even the person he hoped to meet this afternoon. That could be important."

"Well, there's your clue," she said. "Now we can leave."

"Not yet." I reached over the bed to look inside the brass posts, then checked under the bedspread. Lynda observed and did likewise. No secrets there.

While Lynda went into the closet area just inside the door, I attacked the dresser, a reproduction Queen Somebody that was clearly a few cuts above the usual Formica-topped furniture in the motels where I stay during my infrequent road trips for the college. The only thing in the top drawer was a Book, courtesy of the Gideon Society.

I paged through to see if maybe it had been hollowed out and something slipped inside. Clever idea, if I do say so myself, but unfruitful.

"It would help a lot if we knew what we were looking for," Lynda said from the depths of the closet.

"I'm hoping we'll know it when we see it." Max Cutter always does.

The next drawer held underwear and socks neatly folded and stacked by the dead man. There was something pathetic about that, something that touched me more than actually seeing Matheson's bloodied body.

"Here it is!" Lynda called. "Get over here."

In seconds I was at her side. Inside the closet area she had the spare blanket from the overhead rack spread out on the floor, kneeling over it.

"I just unfolded it and found these tucked inside," she said, holding up a faded red book and a fat sheaf of handwritten manuscript pages.

I took the manuscript first, instinctively holding it with respect. At the top of the first page was a chapter heading, "Mr. Sherlock Holmes," and then the beginning of the story:

"Mr. Sherlock Holmes, who was usually very late in the mornings . . ."

What I had in my hands was the opening pages of *The Hound of the Baskervilles* set down as Arthur Conan Doyle wrote them in his own hand. All of the millions of copies of the book that had been printed in all the languages of the world had started with this. As a writer myself, I was moved by that.

I set the pages down and picked up the red volume. It, too, was the *Hound* and I knew what it had to be. Sure enough, there on the title page was an inscription in the same cramped handwriting of the manuscript:

To my dear Robinson—with thanks for the ripping good idea
that put Holmes back in action.
      A.C.D.

"This seals it," I said. "Matheson was the thief, all
right."

"But who killed him?" Lynda said.

I intended to find out.

Chapter Seventeen
Going Home Again

We put the books back where we found them. We were halfway out the door in some haste before I remembered what Max Cutter never would have forgotten—fingerprints. I stepped back in and spent a fast two minutes applying my handkerchief to every surface we had touched.

Downstairs we unchained my bike from the NO PARKING sign in front of the hotel and tied it on top of the Mustang.

In the car, I tried to come to grips with the idea of Hugh Matheson as a thief—and such a small-scale thief by the standards of his huge net worth. Valuable as it was, it was a pittance for a guy who owned three homes in different cities and four antique Duesenberg roadsters.

"It made sense all along in one way, because he was the only big-time Holmes collector on the scene," I mused aloud. "But he was so rich and successful. Why would he risk all that to steal something that was worth less than his take on just one good lawsuit?"

"Ego and lust, I guess," Lynda said. "I was around enough to see both of those."

I studied Lynda's pretty profile. "You really didn't like him, did you?"

"No. He was too full of himself. For that I actually felt kind of sorry for him, though. Still do."

By this time we were sitting in front of the last pay phone in downtown Erin, which looks like the TARDIS in *Doctor Who*. I got out of the car and called 911 to report a disturbance at the Winfield. "It was a noise, almost like a shot," I told the dispatcher who answered, talking in a squeaky voice unlike my own. "It seemed to come out of room 943."

"Did you call the hotel desk?"

"Just check it out."

"Where are you calling from, sir?"

From the TARDIS, lady. Fortunately, I saw a trap in the question. Wouldn't 911 have industrial strength Caller ID? I hung up.

Back on the road, mentally going over all that had happened, I was struck by a glaring omission.

"The third book," I told Lynda. "What was it? Oh, yeah, that Christmas annual with the first Sherlock Holmes story. Why wasn't it with the other books?"

"That's easy," Lynda said without taking her eyes off the road. "The killer took it."

"But why just that one book?"

"Maybe he'd only gotten that far when he heard me starting to come in the door."

"Okay, then how did he—"

"Or she," Lynda added.

"—get out of the room. Unless . . ."

Lynda darted a glance at me. "Yeah. Unless she or he never left. We didn't get around to checking out the bathroom."

"So for all we know the killer could have been just a few feet away the whole time we were in the hotel room. There's a creepy thought for you."

Right away I had another thought as well: If that scenario had actually happened, then the killer would be as late for the banquet as we were. I wanted to drive straight there and check out the crowd, but Lynda insisted on continuing to her apartment first.

"I've got to change my clothes and redo my hair," she said. "I'm as eager to get back to Muckerheide as you are, Jeff, but I described my whole outfit for the evening to Kate. If I don't show up dressed that way, she'll wonder why. Besides, I need a shower. After what we've been through, it's the only way I'll feel, I don't know, *clean* again."

I argued the point all the way to her place, but she was the one driving and I didn't want to leave her any more than she wanted to leave me.

Lynda's apartment is on the second story of a two-family home in a comfortable Erin neighborhood of wide lanes and big trees. I mean comfortable the way your favorite piece of old clothing is comfortable—nothing fancy, it just feels right. The house is brick and stucco, with three gables and a small octagon-shaped room on the first floor. Its owners have lived there since 1974, and they bought it from the wife's parents.

While Lynda cleaned up, I sat on her wicker couch and looked around, feeling as if I'd come home again after a long absence. Not that I was even on first base again with Lynda, but at least I was no longer in the dugout. The room hadn't changed much in the few weeks of my exile from her life: tall bookcase, overflowing with books; a couple of wicker chairs on either side of the bricked-up fireplace; flat-screen TV above the mantle; brass spittoon with sunflowers poking out of it; wicker and glass coffee table. But the picture of Lynda and me on the mantle was gone, along with the stuffed frog holding a red heart that I'd given her for Valentine's Day one year.

Stifling a mad impulse to pick up a sunflower and play "she loves me, she loves me not," which wouldn't have worked too well considering that they were artificial, I forced my mind back to what we'd done in Matheson's hotel room. It had seemed the right thing to do at the time, but now I wasn't at all sure. First of all, if our actions ever came out, we would look guilty as hell. Plus, we'd been in such a hurry to get out of there we might have left the murderer behind. Not that I was really *sorry* we hadn't encountered the armed killer, I admitted to myself gloomily.

How differently Mac would have reacted, I thought. The big man would have been in his element, playing the role of amateur sleuth to the hilt with never a sick feeling in the pit of *his* stomach. And then at some point he would have pulled a rabbit out of his hat, leaving me feeling like a fool for not even knowing he had a hat, much less a rabbit.

Mac had known all along that Matheson was the thief. Or at least he'd *said* he knew the identity of the thief. With him you can never tell when he's just blowing smoke. Even now I didn't understand Mac's hocus-pocus about the keys to Hearth Room C—those questions that he'd asked Decker. Not that it made any difference, of course. Still—

I pulled out my phone and called Decker's office. He was gone for the day, so I tapped the home number next to his photo on my contacts list.

"Cody," the lieutenant growled by way of greeting. "Don't you ever quit working, for crap's sake? It's nearly seven-thirty."

"Thank you, Big Ben. I want to know what you found out about that key to the room where the Holmes books were stolen. Was it shiny?"

"I already told McCabe that—"

"Tell me, damn it."

"—it wasn't."

Okay. Now I knew the answer to the question, but I still didn't know what it meant. "So what the . . ."

"A real cute idea McCabe had, it just didn't work out. Phil Oakland—you know, the locksmith over on Spring Street—he tells me that when a key's been copied it gets shiny on top. Based on that, it looks like neither key to Hearth Room C was copied."

And both of them were accounted for on Friday, so they couldn't have been used by the thief. That was an interesting fact. Maybe it was a semi-good thing that the keying system in Muckerheide was a decade or two overdue for a security update, unlike the one at the Winfield Hotel. Before I had a chance to digest Decker's information any further, I heard Lynda's bathroom door open.

"Thanks, Ed," I said in a rush. I disconnected and put the phone back in my pocket.

But it was eternity before Lynda made her appearance. When she did, the sight of her almost made me forget to breathe. She was decked out in a dress with a vaguely Victorian air, creamy satin with lots of white lace, and not even her ankles peaking out at the bottom. It was as feminine a garment as I'd ever seen, accentuating Lynda's curves—which are considerable—while revealing nothing. The contrast of the dress against her dark complexion was stunning. Lynda paused in the doorway, one hand upon the frame like a countess in a painting.

"You look great, Lyn," I said, a catch in my voice. I used to call her that sometimes, but not for a while.

The painting came to life as she moved out of the doorway. "Sorry it took so long. It was the hair. This isn't just once-over-lightly. It takes time."

"You should wear it like that more often. I mean, if you want to." *See, I'm not bossy.*

Lynda had swept her hair off her face, clipped it with pins, and supplemented it at the back by a chignon bun tied with a lace bow. Curly tendrils framed her face. She wore a cameo on a black ribbon around her throat, which I found quite fetching.

I stood up and moved close enough to hear her heart beat—or maybe it was mine, pounding in my ears. To my surprise she put her arms around me and hugged me, not in passion but in search of comfort. In heels, she was almost my height. The seductive scent of Cleopatra VII, Lynda's favorite fragrance and mine, made my legs weak.

"How do you feel?" I whispered.

"Better," she said. "Not good, but better. I could really use a stiff bourbon on the rocks, though." One of her favorite blogs is called *Bourbon Babe*.

"Sorry. No time for Knob Creek. Besides, you're driving."

"I keep remembering—"

"Try not to," I said.

Session Three

The President's Dining Room

6:30   Reception
        Hors d'oeuvres and cash bar

7:30   Banquet
        Sherlockian sing-along
        Traditional toasts
        Roast beef and Yorkshire pudding
        Awards for best costumes—Kate McCabe

9:00   Reader's Theatre
        "The Adventure of Charles Augustus
        Milverton"—Directed by Dr. Sebastian
        McCabe, BSI

Chapter Eighteen
Costume Party

We captured the last two seats open at Mac's table in the President's Dining Room. It was as if he had been waiting for us.

My brother-in-law was dressed in a brown and tan checked suit with short lapels, a buff-colored waistcoat, an old-fashioned stiff collar and a big tie. The only thing missing was a bowler hat, and he probably had that on his lap or someplace close. He looked up from tucking into his roast beef as we pulled out our chairs.

"Jefferson! Lynda!" he said. "What a delight to see you. I am afraid, however, that you have entirely missed the Sherlockian sing-along and the traditional toasts."

"I'll get over it," I murmured.

"Sorry we're late," Lynda said.

Renata Chalmers leaned over to her. "The hair always takes longer than you think, doesn't it?"

Lynda answered with a polite and meaningless affirmative, never mind that homicide had a lot more to do with her tardiness than did hair care. Renata herself was wearing her hair in fancy ringlets, the creation of which, she informed us, had caused her to miss the entire cocktail hour.

"Still," she said, "dressing up was fun."

The rest of Renata's outfit, like Mac's, was suitably Victorian—a dark blue-green dress with a short fitted jacket on top. The sleeves of the jacket were puffed at the shoulders and tapered at the wrists where they ended in a frilly, cream-colored cloth. The blouse was also cream, topped with a black bow around the neck.

Lynda complimented her on it, generating a lively discussion of Victorian fashion. But while most of the table was talking bustles and bowlers, Mac whispered in my ear, "Please report on your discussion with Mr. Post."

"The hell I will," I whispered back. "I'm not your errand boy."

"Jefferson, I said 'please.'"

"Oh, all right. There's not much to tell, anyway. Post is an arrogant stuffed shirt, but I'm convinced he had nothing to do with the theft either before or after the fact. That interview was a wash-out, just like your cute idea about duplicating the key to the room where the books were stolen."

Mac looked at me with infinite sadness in his brown eyes. "The key was only a hope; I never really believed it would prove to be the solution."

A waitress hustled by with my roast beef, and the mood was broken. By the time she disappeared again Mac was engaged in the general conversation and I'd lost him. I picked at my dinner—I try not to eat too much red meat—and looked around the room getting a fix on familiar faces. Kate was at our table, of course, dressed in an enchanting black velvet dress with a high collar and silver buttons up to the top. I was only vaguely aware of two other couples next to her, people who were unfamiliar to me. Around the room I saw that Judge Crocker and Dr. Queensbury were in costume, but Al Kane and Bob Nakamora weren't. And Woollcott Chalmers . . .

Dressed in tails, Chalmers was just now coming toward our table, limping badly without his cane.

I kicked my brother-in-law under the table. He grunted and inclined his head in my direction.

"Has Chalmers been out of the picture since this banquet business started?" I asked in an urgent whisper.

Mac guffawed, causing Lynda to visibly strain her ears our way. "By no means, Jefferson. We spent the entire cocktail hour together in a spirited discussion of chronological problems in 'The Red-Headed League.' He is merely returning from a short hiatus, undoubtedly provoked by the demands of personal biology. Why do you ask?"

"I'm taking a census." Max Cutter could play mysterious sleuth as well as any amateur. For once I knew something Mac didn't know, and I was going to play that out as long as I could. "Is there somebody else here who wasn't here at the beginning, somebody who came in late?" The killer didn't have to be one of the Sherlockians, but it was a good bet.

Mac pulled on his beard, as if stimulating his hair follicles would do the same for his brain cells.

"There is at least one person," he decided. "Hugh Matheson. I haven't encountered him for hours, not even at the bar."

Others around the table heard the comment and nodded their agreement. Nobody had run into Matheson since just after the last session of the colloquium—except, of course, Lynda and me, and we weren't saying.

"I am quite certain that the last time I saw Hugh was during his set-to with Noah," Mac said just as Chalmers rejoined the table.

"He had an argument with Queensbury?" I said. "When? Where?"

"At the back of the room, right after Kate's talk," Chalmers chipped in.

"What were they arguing about?"

Chalmers shrugged his ignorance.

"Eavesdropping is a loathsome habit," Mac said. "Perhaps you should inquire of Dr. Queensbury as to the nature of the contretemps."

"In other words," I said, "you couldn't get close enough to hear and you're annoyed."

He didn't deign to answer. I let the subject hang there, hoping somebody would pick it up and enlighten me on what had happened between the surgeon and the lawyer, but no one did. The conversation drifted off into other channels.

Somehow the topic got on to Sherlock Holmes in the movies. Names like Basil Rathbone, Arthur Wontner, Jeremy Brett, and Robert Downey, Jr., and somebody named Cumberbatch were bandied about, along with a bunch I don't remember. I was familiar with Basil Rathbone—he looked like Queensbury—and I'd also seen a couple of the Brett TV shows and the over-the-top Robert Downey, Jr. movie. But the other names left me in the dust. It was like being on the outside of an inside joke. I was only half-listening anyway.

While it was going hot and heavy Mac leaned my way again, hand over his mouth. "Are you going to tell me what this is all about?" he demanded in a low voice.

"No," I said absent-mindedly.

My mind was on the dust-up between Queensbury and Hugh Matheson, a man who stopped breathing no more than an hour or so later. Lynda and I had been assuming that greed was the emotion behind the murder, a robbery gone wrong. But suppose there was some other passion involved—whatever had caused those two men to raise their voices in a public place.

I watched for Queensbury to leave the table where he was seated next to Molly Crocker, determined to question him as soon as possible. When my bladder started crying for relief I ignored it, afraid I'd miss a chance to corner Queensbury if I left the President's Dining Room. Finally the tall surgeon made a bee-line for the exit, apparently in a big hurry. I excused myself to Lynda and followed him.

Into the men's room.

Now I was glad I had a legitimate reason for being there. Once I took care of that I met Queensbury at the wash basins. He greeted me as an old friend while he washed his long-fingered hands. Before I could ask a question he offered his solution to the book thefts.

"It's that Pfannenstiel fellow," he said, a gleam in his gray eyes. "There was no sign of a forced entry because there was no forced entry. The thief used a key. Who had a key? The very person who set up the exhibit with the Chalmerses. Elementary, really."

"I don't believe it," I said, holding my hands under the hot air blower. "Not Gene."

"As Holmes himself said, 'when you have eliminated the impossible, whatever remains, *however improbable*, must be the truth.' Something similar happened at the University of Pennsylvania in 1990. A part-time library employee was charged with stealing more than a hundred rare books with a total value of almost a million and a half dollars. I clipped the story for my scrapbooks."

I knew that Gene couldn't be guilty because Matheson was—unless, of course, Gene had been Matheson's inside man. But in that case why stop at three books? With Gene's access they could have practically loaded up a truck and cleaned the place out.

I shifted gears.

"I understand you had a bit of a confrontation with Hugh Matheson this afternoon."

With a shrug of his shoulders, the surgeon pooh-poohed that description of the incident. "I guess you'd say we had a few heated words, as usual."

"What was it about?"

"He accused me of spoiling the colloquium for him by insisting at every turn that Sherlock Homes was a real person," Queensbury said as he pushed open the restroom door. "Apparently the last straw was when I stood up at the end of Kate's talk to dispute her attribution of Conan Doyle as the author of the Holmes stories.

"Really, Hugh was intolerably rude about it and totally lacking in humor. I particularly objected to his characterization of me as, quote, 'a prissy piss-ant.' However, I gave the fellow the benefit of the doubt. Perhaps he was having a bad day."

Remembering the sight of the lawyer's blood-drenched body, I could confirm that. But I didn't, of course.

"The exchange was heated and rather loud," Queensbury continued, "but it only lasted a few moments before Hugh said he didn't have any more time for such foolishness. He was in a hurry."

"Did he say why?"

"Oh, yes. He was rather gleeful about it. He told me with a distinct leer that he had business with a lady."

Chapter Nineteen
Oscar the Grouch

"A lady?" Lynda repeated later, almost hissing the words. "That was me!" she exclaimed ungrammatically.

"Shhh. I know that—and you don't have to tell everybody else." We were standing at the back of the President's Dining Room. Mac was at the front, saying something about the upcoming Reader's Theatre. "The point here, Lynda, is that Queensbury might share that little tidbit with the police. And if he does, and if the police find out you were Matheson's constant companion at the colloquium today, you can expect Oscar to land on you like a ton of bricks."

"Oscar Hummel *is* a ton of bricks."

"He's a little overweight." Maybe sixty pounds or so, not closer to a hundred like Mac. "He's also made his share of high-profile goofs, but don't underestimate him—especially his tenacity. That would be a big mistake."

"He has all the subtlety of a suicide bomber."

"Yeah," I agreed, "and he could be just as destructive."

We reclaimed our seats as the Reader's Theatre began. Some local acting talent, including a few students, sat on stools at the front of the room and took parts reading a Sherlock Holmes story, "The Adventure of Charles Augustus Milverton." They wore only symbolic costumes—Holmes was identified by the ubiquitous deerstalker cap, for example. There were two Dr. Watsons—one the narrator and one the character—and both wore bowlers.

The title character of the story, Milverton, is the Worst Man in London, Holmes tells Watson. He is trying to squeeze blackmail out of a female client of Holmes, who refuses to play ball. Instead, Holmes adopts the identity of a plumber and romances Milverton's housemaid. Once he wheedles enough information out of her, he cons Watson into helping him burgle Milverton's house late one night to retrieve a set of embarrassing letters.

Holmes and Watson had just entered the grounds of the Milverton estate when Erin's Finest came into the President's Dining Room.

The beer belly alone might have been enough to make me recognize him out of the corner of my eye, but the headgear eliminated all doubt. Who else in Erin, Ohio, would wear a Panama hat? It had to be Oscar Hummel, a man too vain to show his balding head in public and yet too cheap to buy a wig. He always covers his pate with some tasteless hat or cap.

He sidled up to Mac, who was standing at the front of the room in his role as director of the Reader's Theatre. After a tête-à-tête of no more than thirty seconds, the two left the room together, going past our table on the way out.

"What do you think Oscar wants with Mac?" Lynda asked in a low voice.

"You can bet they aren't talking baseball," I said. "Oscar probably found out from the Winfield that Matheson was in Erin for the colloquium. Mac organized the colloquium, so he might know the guy, right? Remember, Oscar has a keen perception of the obvious."

That's what had me worried. Of course Oscar would have his men scour the hotel for witnesses, just as any big-city force would do. How long could it be before somebody remembered seeing a man and woman leaving the hotel or maybe even Matheson's floor around the time of the killing? Hours, not days. I had visions of Oscar throwing Lynda and me in his basement cell and shining lights in our eyes. Suddenly it was hot in the President's Dining Room.

The actors on the stools in front were winding down their presentation of "The Adventure of Charles Augustus Milverton." Holmes and Watson, nearly caught in the act of burglary, watch as Milverton meets with one of his blackmail victims, a mysterious woman. She pulls out a gun and plugs Milverton repeatedly. With the rest of the household awakened by gunfire, Holmes and Watson run for it. (I kind of knew how they felt.) The out-of-shape doctor barely makes it over the wall and then—

I felt a tap on my shoulder.

My body twitched and I sucked air.

"Man, Jeff, you got a guilty conscience or what?"

"Oscar!" I said. "What are you doing here?"

"Tell you in the hallway."

Oscar Hummel is forty-seven years old and looks older, never been married and it shows. Sometimes I worry that he's what I could become in another few years of bachelorhood, minus the belly, but then I remind myself that I have better clothes sense. He was wearing a plaid sport coat over hound's tooth pants and a pink shirt, no tie.

I followed him and Lynda followed me. Mac was a few yards outside the door, sitting in a blue plastic chair and making a half-dollar appear and disappear in his oversized hands.

"Cut out the damned parlor tricks," Oscar growled at him. Turning to say something to me, he finally caught on that Lynda was part of the entourage.

"Oh, joy," he said. "The press. Just what I need at nine-thirty on a Saturday night when I oughta be popping a beer and watching the Reds in spring training."

"The game was this afternoon," Lynda said. "They played the Cubs. I don't know who won."

Oscar didn't seem to be particularly cheered by this information. He sighed. "At least you can give me a cigarette, Teal." His mother disapproves of him smoking, so Oscar never buys cigarettes. But that doesn't stop him from smoking them. This time, however, Lynda shook her head. "Sorry, Chief, I quit."

He favored her with a sour look. "In that case, get the hell out of here."

"What's going on?" I asked, just as if I didn't know.

Lynda, ignoring Oscar's order to leave, silently offered him a stick of Big Red. He took it without thanks.

"Murder," he said, putting the gum into his mouth. "Hot-shot lawyer from Cincy. Hugh Matheson. I've heard of him—who hasn't?—and Mac knew him."

"Indeed," Mac said, making the coin vanish with the slightest motion of his hand. "The news of Hugh's passing in this unpleasant manner is most distressing."

"We weren't friends," I told Oscar, "but I met him this weekend."

"And I sat next to him during some of the lectures and at lunch," Lynda volunteered. *Very smart, pointing that out before somebody else does.*

Oscar grimaced and took the gum out of his mouth. "I hate cinnamon. Are you trying to poison me or what, Teal?"

"Don't talk like that," I snapped. The murder had me about ready to jump out of my skin, and I certainly was in no mood for attempts at homicidal humor.

"What happened to Matheson?" Lynda asked Oscar, another smart move on her part.

"Shot in the neck. Hit an artery, spouted blood all over the place."

"Where did it happen?" Lynda persisted in her best journalist voice.

"In his room at the Winfield. Somebody called 911 with an anonymous tip around seven o'clock.Enough with

the questions, Teal. We already got enough of that from
your man Silverstein. He picked up the dispatch on the
scanner and got there even before my people did—made a
nuisance out of himself as usual."

"That's my Ben."

"Do you have any ideas about this anonymous
caller?" I tried to sound only casually interested.

Oscar shrugged. "The call came from a pay phone
not too far from the hotel. I haven't listened to the
recording yet but the dispatcher said it was a man talking in
a high-pitched voice, like Minnie Mouse on helium."
Smartass. "I figure it must have been somebody who was
almost desperate to not get involved, maybe somebody
whose wife didn't know he was at the hotel."

Mac caressed his beard. "You are confident it
wasnot the killer?" *Thanks a heap, Mac.*

"That wouldn't make a lot of sense from the killer's
point of view, Mac. The sooner law enforcement gets to the
scene of a homicide, the better. It would have helped the
killer if the body hadn't been found until tomorrow. As it
was, we got there less than half an hour after the shooting."

Oops. I'd unintentionally misled the police about
the time of the murder, but it couldn't have been by all that
much; the blood was still fresh when we arrived around six-
thirty.

"Where do I come into this?" I asked.

Mac said, "I persuaded Oscar that you should be
involved in your capacity as public relations director for the
college. The murder investigation is likely to spill over onto
the campus grounds, given Matheson's reason for being in
Erin."

"He didn't say anything about Teal tagging along,"
Oscar added.

"Consider me a bonus," she said.

Applause erupted from inside the closed doors of
the President's Dining Room. If I remembered the agenda

correctly, Kate must have been announcing the winners of the costume contest.

"As a working premise," Mac said, "what do you think happened, Oscar?"

"Well . . . this is strictly off the record, Teal, understand?"

"Yes, massa," Lynda said.

"It must have been somebody who knew him, not a homicide committed during a burglary. There was no break-in, for one thing, and it doesn't look like anything was disturbed."

Give Lynda and me points for neatness.

"Besides," Oscar added, "we have a witness, another guest at the Winfield, who saw the victim open the door for someone who may have been the killer."

Damn—just what I had feared. Somebody saw Lynda coming out of the room and me standing there. We must have given quite a show, the big hug. The pit of my stomach felt like a load of concrete had been mixed there. I shot a covert glance at Lynda. She swallowed hard.

"A witness!" Mac bellowed. "Oh, Oscar, you are the sly one, holding that back. Tell us about this witness."

The chief allowed himself a self-satisfied smirk.

"She's rock solid—an IRS attorney in town to check out the college for her daughter," Oscar said. "She came back to her room down the hall to take a shower around six and saw Matheson open the door to a visitor. She didn't see the visitor's face, but get this: He was wearing one of those funny Sherlock Holmes hats. What do you call them?"

"A deerstalker," I said in a choked voice, nearly limp with relief.

Maybe it really *was* the killer this witness saw—it sure wasn't Lynda. Aside from the chapeau she wasn't wearing, the timing was off by half an hour. We weren't even finished with Post by six o'clock.

"Yeah, that's it—a deerstalker," Oscar said. "I figure it should be easy to find this character. How many people can there be running around Erin in a deerstalker hat?"

Chapter Twenty
What We Have Here . . . (Part Two)

Mac's answer to Oscar was a sound that started as a rumble in his stomach and burst forth from his lips as a hearty, uncontrolled laugh.

"What the hell's so funny?" Oscar demanded.

"Deerstalker caps," Lynda said, "are about as rare at this little confab as big ears on an elephant."

Standing between Mac and Oscar, no wonder she thought of elephants. Oscar glowered at her.

"Surely you understand what this colloquium is all about, Oscar?" Mac said. Without waiting for an answer, he added, "Unfortunately, this isn't the only crime that has marred an otherwise delightful occasion. Do you suppose there could be a link between the theft last night of several rare Sherlock Holmes volumes and the murder of Hugh Matheson?"

"Well," Oscar said heavily, "there sure as hell seems to be some kind of connection to Sherlock Holmes."

But Oscar didn't know what the link was—his officers apparently hadn't found the hidden books in Matheson's hotel room.

"Obviously, you're going to be conducting some interviews around here tomorrow," I said. "I'd appreciate it if you would check in with Ed Decker, let him know what you're up to. You know how touchy he is about turf issues."

Oscar grunted, which I took to be an affirmative response. "If you remember anything that might be important about the victim, give me a call. You have my cell."

"I'm sure I'll be in touch," Lynda said, earning a malevolent stare from the chief.

"Good night, Oscar," Mac said. "And thank you for the flower."

"The what?"

Mac reached into Oscar's plaid sport coat and pulled a carnation out of the inside pocket. He affixed it to the lapel of his Victorian suit coat while Oscar watched with an expression composed of equal parts surprise and chagrin.

"You ought to stick to magic," Oscar told Mac. "You're good at it. Leave the detective work to law enforcement."

With a curt nod to each of us he disappeared down the escalator.

"I'd better go, too," Lynda said. "I've got to get to the office and help Ben with his story for the website and tomorrow's paper."

Mac and I wished her good night. It was ten o'clock and I felt a deep weariness, as if I'd been up for at least three days. And, like Lynda, I still had work to do.

"I'd better call Ralph and get it over with," I told Mac with a sigh of resignation.

"You have my sympathy," he said.

"I need it. But it would be even worse if Ralph heard it someplace else first. Never let your boss be surprised."

I pulled out my phone, chose Ralph's name from my contacts list, and tapped his phone number.

"This is Jeff Cody," I said when the provost had answered in his precise voice. I could hear music playing in the background. *Could that really be Dave Brubeck?* "You aren't going to like this."

"That I believe. Well, what is it now?"

"One of the participants in this Sherlock Holmes colloquium thing has been murdered."

"Good God in heaven!"

I winced and pulled the phone away from my ear. The expression on Mac's hairy face showed that he'd heard Ralph almost as well as I had.

"It isn't as if the body showed up in the middle of Muckerheide Center," I said quickly. "The murder was off-campus."

"Thank God for that. Give me the details." I could have sworn Ralph had stopped to drink something between the two sentences.

I summed up the case as Oscar knew it—leaving out, of course, what I knew that the chief didn't.

"What we have here, Ralph," I concluded, "is a very unfortunate set of circumstances, especially with the murder following the theft so closely. But I'm on top of it. I've spent quite a bit of time discussing this case with the chief of police. I'm sure that when he finds this mysterious visitor in the deerstalker the murder will be solved."

"And I suppose we can look forward to yet another spate of unfavorable publicity when someone is arrested," Ralph said. "At least it isn't likely to be a college employee. Is it?" The last two words came out almost as a plea.

The doors of the President's Dining Room swung open. Sherlockians spilled out in a sea of now-familiar faces—Molly Crocker, the deerstalkered (yes!) Dr. Queensbury, Sven Larsen, Professor Whippet . . .

"Well, Cody?"

I went as far as I could, assuring Ralph that neither Mac nor I nor anybody connected with St. Benignus College had been wearing a deerstalker cap today.

"What you have to do is downplay the college connection with this so-called colloquium," said Ralph, who had made a speech earlier that day accepting the Woollcott

Chalmers Collection as a highlight of what he now dismissed as the "so-called colloquium."

I promised him I'd use all my influence with the police and the press. It was an easy promise because I have none. But it mollified Ralph, who believes otherwise.

"I suppose your intentions are good, Cody," he conceded. "I might even be able to make something out of you if you weren't under the constant influence of the execrable McCabe."

The thought had been expressed before, and not just by Ralph. It's undeniably true that my life would be simpler and less turbulent without Sebastian McCabe in it. But it would be a lot less interesting, too.

"Mac's right here," I told Ralph. "Want to talk to him?" There I went again, showing that constant influence.

"Spare me, Cody. I'm warning you, if you can't get control of this story I'll find someone who can."

He hung up.

"Good show!" Mac said. "That was a most convincing performance, old boy, just then and earlier with Oscar as well. Now perhaps you would care to give me the unexpurgated version."

"Meaning what?"

"Meaning," Mac said, making a show of studying his unlighted cigar, "the whole story of your personal involvement in the murder—the details of which you did not share with Oscar for quite good reasons, no doubt."

Chapter Twenty-One
Too Many Suspects

"How do you figure—"

"Hell and damnation, Jefferson," my brother-in-law thundered, "do not trifle with me at a time like this! I cannot pretend I knew instantly the reason for your strong interest earlier in Hugh Matheson's argument with Noah Queensbury. I would be doltish indeed, however, if I did not see the implications of it now. That, coupled with your late arrival, your question about who else arrived late, and your sly looks at Ms. Teal—congratulations on your rapprochement with her, incidentally—all make the conclusion inescapable: You are in this mess up to your red eyebrows."

I raised my hands in protest, speaking quickly as Kate and the Chalmerses appeared among the crowd in the doorway of the President's Dining Room. "It's not like I killed the guy or anything, but it'll look bad if Oscar finds out I'm the one who called 911 and didn't leave my name. I could say I didn't have time to tell you about it, but the truth is I wanted to leave you out of it for your own good."

"People have been trying to do things for my own good all of my life," Mac said. "Fortunately, I have thus far managed to frustrate them at every turn."

With my sister and Mac's friends almost within earshot, we agreed to discuss the matter later at his house. Mac hobnobbed with the other Sherlockians until they'd all disappeared to their own homes or hotel rooms, then piled me and his house guests into his oversized Chevy.

At Mac's house we checked out the eleven o'clock news to see if the Cincinnati TV stations had picked up the murder of the city's most famous lawyer. At the same time I was surfing the news websites on my iPhone. Ben and Lynda's story wasn't on the web yet, and only Channel 9 had a sketchy "this just in" report of about ten seconds near the end of the newscast. But TV4 used a full two minutes on the colloquium and the Woollcott Chalmers Collection. After a few seconds of me talking about the theft, it focused mostly on Chalmers using his cane to point out the wax bust of Sherlock Holmes and various other highlights of the Sherlockiana display.

It must have been midnight by the time the others went to bed, leaving Mac and me to adjourn to his study. Here I must explain that the study of Sebastian McCabe is a wonderful working room, a large one, not a *House Beautiful* model of decorating. It has books on all four walls, sure. But it also has the computer he writes on, a bar with a beer tap, and a big-screen TV. When the Big One gets dropped and humanity has to stay indoors for few generations, that's where I want to be. It's my favorite room in all the world.

I commandeered a comfortable leather chair while Mac tapped himself a Cincinnati microbrewcalled Christian Moerlein OTR Ale into a frosted mug.

"Do not just tell me what happened," he directed. "Re-live your adventures. Spare no details."

I gave him everything I could remember, right down to the conversation with Queensbury in the men's room. Okay, I left out the hugs with Lynda because I saw no reason to appeal to his prurient interest. But I gave him everything else.

"You," Mac said at the conclusion, "are in great peril. And Lynda with you. Pardon the detective story cliché, but if we fail to unmask the murderer without undue delay, Oscar is going to reach his own conclusion and it won't be pretty."

"Wow, you really are a Great Detective."

"Sarcasm is the lowest form of humor, Jefferson, below even puns. As to your actions, I must say that blundering around in the murder room, then concealing it from Oscar as though you had some personal culpability to hide, really was remarkably dense."

"It seemed a good idea at the time," I mumbled, steamed that he was right.

Mac drank deeply of his beer and stuck an unlighted cigar in his mouth.

"Besides," I added, "at least we found the books."

"Ah, yes. And what do you see as the importance of that?"

"Well, now we know that Matheson stole the books, of course—the last salvo in his ongoing feud with Chalmers."

"What became of the third missing volume, the *Beeton's Christmas Annual*?"

"How should I know?" I pried my eyes open and stifled a yawn, all-too-aware that my brain was on low speed at best. "Maybe the killer took it for a souvenir. Who knows what somebody wearing a deerstalker might do?"

"Then you accept Oscar's assumption that the earlier visitor to Hugh's room was the killer?"

I hesitated. "It's a good working theory, at least."

"Agreed."

"So then all we have to do is find the person beneath the hat?"

"Indeed. That task may be simple to state but not necessarily easy to accomplish, however. There are many possibilities and many people who should be interviewed. Take out your notebook, please." Without thinking, I did so. "Write down these names: Gene Pfannenstiel, Molly Crocker—"

"Hold it." I stopped with my pen halfway through 'Pfannenstiel.' "I'm not your Watson—or your secretary."

"And quite a good thing," Mac commented, drawing another beer. His administrative assistant, Heidi Guildenstern, is an insufferable woman whom I have long suspected of being a spy for Ralph Pendergast. "I prefer to think of you as my amanuensis."

Later, I looked that up in a dictionary and found out it out means "one employed to take dictation," coming from the Latin word for a slave acting as a secretary. But even that night in Mac's comfortable man-cave, before I knew exactly what the word meant, I resented it because it was a big word I didn't know the meaning of.

I handed Mac the notebook and pen. "Do it yourself, genius."

"Really, Jefferson," he said with a sigh, "you can at times be remarkably petty and stubborn." *Oh, you think so, too.* For the record, I prefer to think of myself as determined, not stubborn.

Despite his feeble protest, Mac wrote a bunch of names and handed the notebook back to me. I looked at the list:

Gene Pfannenstiel
Molly Crocker
Noah Queensbury
Graham Bentley Post
Woollcott Chalmers
Renata Chalmers
Reuben Pinkwater
The person whose phone number was on the notepad in Hugh's room

"Who's this Reuben Pinkwater?" I asked.

"A book dealer from Licking Falls. Undoubtedly you've seen his display at the colloquium."

"The bald guy? Yeah, I've seen him."

Maybe Matheson had been killed for the missing book after all. But how would this Pinkwater know Matheson was the thief? And why hadn't he taken the other two books? After a little sleep I'd probably have other questions, but right now I could think of just one more:

"Do you really consider all of these people suspects?"

"By no means," Mac said. "A few are merely individuals who might have seen or heard something of significance."

"You're going to interview all of them?"

Mac's bushy eyebrows, both of them this time, shot up as if he were astounded at the notion. "Of course not, old boy! You are."

I was reduced to inarticulate noises.

"How would I have time to interview any of them, much less all?" Mac continued. "I have duties as host of the colloquium. Surely you are more than capable of formulating the proper questions for each to elicit enlightening responses?"

That was really playing dirty. How could I say no? But I didn't give in right away. I threw the notebook on a small table near my chair and we discussed it. The discussion ended with me saying, "I'm not doing it for you. This is my own investigation for my own good. I just hope I can put the finger on somebody before Oscar finds another witness that saw Lynda and me leaving the murder room. Anyone'll do, so long as he's guilty."

"Ah, the Max Cutter approach," Mac observed.

"Maybe I can get Lynda to help. Her neck is on the line, too."

"Splendid! A fine detective duo you two would make, in the grand tradition of Nick and Nora Charles, John Steed and Emma Peel, Fox Mulder and—"

"Oh, shut up," I said, standing. "Just one more thing before I go to bed: Ed Decker said the Hearth Room

C key that's kept in the Muckerheide Center offices wasn't shiny and you said yours wasn't either. That's supposed to be an indication those keys weren't copied; Decker knows that much. So how did Matheson get in without leaving a trace? Do you think Gene helped him?"

"I am quite certain that he did not," Mac said, "and for the best of reasons: Hugh Matheson did not take those books or cause them to be taken or acquire them after they were taken. He was not the thief, nor—I am reasonably certain—did he even know who the thief was."

Chapter Twenty-Two
Public Relations

For hours I lay in bed without sleeping, the day's events churning over and over in my mind as I positioned myself on my right side, my left, my stomach, my back, my right side . . . Eventually I must have nodded off or I wouldn't have had the dream.

Mac and Lynda were there, and so were Woollcott and Renata Chalmers, Judge Molly Crocker and Hugh Matheson. Everybody was running from the Winfield to Muckerheide Center and back again in speeded-up time, like a Keystone Kops movie. Chalmers shook his cane at the others as if in reprimand.

They were all wearing deerstalkers.

Mac had just pulled off Lynda's hairpiece when the Indiana Jones theme song blaring out of the iPhone on the nightstand by my bed shattered the dream. I bolted up, fumbled for the phone, grabbed it, and finally stammered out a hello.

"Jeff? It's Morrie Kindle, Associated Press."

For five years Morrie has been stringing for the AP, and I've known him longer than that, but he always gives me the complete ID.

"You got a crime wave going on there at Benignus or what?" he demanded.

I pulled the phone away from my ear to look at the time: 6:36, the numbers said. By now the print edition of the *ErinObserver& News-Ledger*, which is where Morrie gets

most of his news, would be decorating the front lawns of
Erin. I should have stolen Ralph's.

"I suppose you're calling about the Matheson
murder?" I said.

"Unless there's some other campus crime I should
know about."

My head was pounding from the lack of sleep and
my eyes hurt. I was in no mood for trading witty dialogue
with an untalented scribe.

"I haven't seen the *Observer* and I can't help you
much on this one anyway, Morrie," I snapped. "The murder
didn't happen on campus and Campus Security isn't
involved. I really don't know very much about it." All but
the last sentence was clearly true, and I could make an
argument for the last one. "Why don't you wake up Chief
Hummel and see what he can tell you?"

Morrie assured me that Oscar was next on his call
list. But he had a few questions about "this Sherlock
Holmes deal" that had brought Matheson to Erin. He
already knew something about the colloquium from
rewriting the *Observer* story on the stolen books caper for the
AP, but he wasn't sure where a big shot legal eagle like
Matheson fit into such shenanigans.

"I guess he was crazy," I said, "just like all the other
Sherlockians. That's off the record, of course. But why else
would a grown man collect all that Holmes stuff?"

"He was a collector? You mean like books? Rare
books about Sherlock Holmes?" Morrie Kindle's voice got
louder and faster. I could almost hear his heart go into
overdrive. Even a second-tier reporter could see the story
there. "Still off the record, Jeff, there has to be some kind of
connection between this murder and those books being
taken, don't you think?"

"Off the record, Morrie? I really don't know what to
think."

I meant it. When we'd found the stolen books in the dead man's hotel room it had seemed so clear to Lynda and me that Matheson was the thief. Not so, Sebastian McCabe had insisted—and then refused to elaborate.

When I finally convinced Morrie that I was innocent of any useful thoughts, he hung up on me.

The morning was cool and the sun was hiding. Instead of pulling up erinobserver.com on my smartphone to read the story like a smart public relations director would have, I went into denial mode and tried to hide under the covers. It was no use; sleep wanted no part of me. Finally I gave up and got out of bed. I showered, shaved, and slipped on a pair of khaki slacks and a light blue shirt with thin green lines running in both directions. I would have looked right at home at a boat dock or trendy bar.

Dressed for the day ahead, I retrieved the morning newspaper from the lawn in front of the carriage house and took it back to my apartment to read.

The headline on the top story was informative if not particularly creative: **FAMED LITIGATOR SLAIN AT WINFIELD.** I was impressed that the headline writer got by with using the word "litigator" instead of the shorter "lawyer." A hint of mystery entered the story in the subhead: *Did Killer Wear Deerstalker Cap?*

There was a little refer line in bold type politely telling the reader to *Please see related story, page 12A*. The inside piece turned out to be Lynda's story on the presentation of the Chalmers Collection. It was illustrated by a nice photo of Chalmers and Ralph, who didn't look nearly as constipated as usual, so that was good. But the murder story started at the top of 1A. That's what everybody would read.

With his typical thorough reporting, Bernard J. Silverstein had gotten all the facts straight, as far as the police had known them last night. The third paragraph read:

"Matheson was in Erin, police and hotel officials said, to take part in a colloquium on 'Investigating Arthur Conan Doyle and Sherlock Holmes' being held this weekend at St. Benignus College."

That was the first of four references to the college in the main story. I counted them because I was sure that Ralph Pendergast would.

As the subhead hinted, Ben had really taken off on the Holmes angle again. Who could blame him? The murder of a "famed litigator" in our little town was juicy stuff by itself. Throwing in the stolen books, the colloquium, and the mysterious visitor in the deerstalker made it *National Enquirer* and *Inside Edition* material. It would be an epic, too, and not a one-day wonder. And after the AP story went out, the aforementioned tabloids and their allegedly more respectable brethren in national media would be on it like bees on flowers.

Not that I blamed Lynda, for she was only a news editor doing her job, but how could she do this to me? I crumpled up the first section of the newspaper and threw it across the room at a bookcase, where it knocked over the perfidious woman's photo.

Well, that didn't help matters, even if it did feel good. I had to concentrate on the murder and solve it myself. That was my only chance to limit the journalistic feeding frenzy to a few days. I sat in my armchair and tried to think.

In any good detective story, the killer would be just about anybody who *hadn't* been seen wearing a deerstalker. And it could be that way. It wouldn't have taken much for somebody to borrow one for an hour or so as a sort of slight disguise or protective coloring. But I couldn't help thinking of Noah Queensbury. He'd been dressed in that particular headgear every time I'd seen him. And he'd had an argument with Matheson shortly before the murder. How did I know he was telling the truth when he said they'd been arguing about Sherlock Holmes? Maybe it was something a lot more serious.

But would he really kill somebody? As loony as he seemed, Queensbury was a surgeon.

So was Jack the Ripper, most likely.

The Indiana Jones theme song interrupted my reverie. At least this time I was awake. Reluctantly, I answered the phone with, "Hello, Ralph." I plowed on before he chance to say anything. "I'm sorry about the *Observer* story, but you know there was no way to keep the college out of Matheson's murder."

"Murder? Oh, yes, most regrettable. But what your friend Ms. Teal did with that story about the presentation of the Woollcott Chalmers Collection was even worse."

"Huh?" Blindsided and scrambling to figure out what he was talking about, I quickly un-crumpled the paper. Spreading the relevant page in front of me,I once again looked at the photo of the distinguished Woollcott Chalmers and the un-constipated Ralph Pendergast. The story with it was heavy on adjectives that indicated what an honor this was for St. Benignus College to be the recipient of the collection. Lynda had written it, as well as apparently helping Ben with his page one murder story. "What's wrong with it? I couldn't write a story that positive."

"No doubt," Ralph's dry voice dripped acid. "But if you had interviewed the provost perhaps even you would have quoted *him* in the story, not McCabe."

I sighed."Whose picture is with the story, Ralph?"

He conceded that his was.

"That's worth a thousand words," I said. "College official meets enthusiastic contributor. We'll get permission to put that picture on the website and reprint it in the alumni magazine and in the next fund-raising brochure. It's dynamite."

"Do you really think so, Cody?"

"Scout's honor." I'd never been a Scout, but Ralph didn't know that. He was mollified enough about the Chalmers Collection story to start worrying about the murder again. I promised I'd stick close to the situation all day and do any damage control that might be necessary. By the time Ralph hung up I congratulated myself that I'd avoided another royal ass-chewing.

That happy thought was marred by one of the less pleasing of the sounds that punctuate my life. *Vroooom!* Mac's ancient Chevy was tearing out of the garage below me. I looked out the window just in time to see the tail fins disappearing down the road. The Chalmerses were leaving for the second day of the symposium. Mac again would preside over the day's rather limited activities like a royal duke while he expected me to do his leg work, damn him anyway.

Even worse, I was going to do it.

I called Lynda to enlist her help—I figured she owed me for the morning I'd had so far—but got no answer. Today being Sunday, maybe she was at Mass with her cell phone turned off. I'm not Catholic, but I should have been in church myself, praying my way out of this. (In case anybody is worried about my sister and brother-in-law, who *are* Catholic, they hit the 5:15 p.m. Mass in the chapel the night before.)

Or maybe Lynda was somewhere else. Should I send her a text: *Where the hell are you?* Better not. She would not react well.

As I disconnected the call I looked around for my notebook with Mac's list of suspects—casually at first, then with a growing concern. After a minute of that I realized I must have left it in Mac's study last night. I put on a jacket, picked up my wallet and keys, and went out of my apartment, locking up behind me. With the McCabes gone to the colloquium and the three McCabe children all staying overnight with friends for the weekend, there was nobody to let me into the house. Fortunately I have my own key, which I used.

The notebook was on the small table where I'd thrown it in a pique last night. I stuck it in my pocket and left the study, heading out of the house. Then I stopped, frozen.

I'd heard something—I wasn't sure what, but *something*, a noise in an empty house where there should have been no noise.

Chapter Twenty-Three
Personal Space

With stealth and caution I passed through the hallway toward the guest suite at the back of the house, where the noise had appeared to originate. *Down these mean streets a man must go . . .* Along the way I picked up my nephew Brian's baseball bat from the kitchen. It was only aluminum but it felt comforting in my hand. I held it like a club.

Outside the suite, added on by the previous owners for the wife's parents, I paused. My stomach was one big mass of knots and my heart was pounding in my ears from the adrenaline rush. I wiped sweaty palms on my khaki slacks.

Strangely, from this close up the noise in the suite sounded like water running in the bathroom.

Should I knock first and give the traditional "Who's there?" or should I barge right in, bat at the ready? *WWMD—What Would Max Do?*

Opting for the element of surprise, I tightened my grip on the bat with my right hand and pushed in the doorknob with my left. And I walked in.

The empty bedroom was large and bright, with sun pouring in from a window overlooking a spectacular view of the Ohio River. There were two dressers opposite the bed (one of them with a mirror), a clothes tree draped with clothes, a couple of modern lamps and a captain's chair. At the far end of the room, to the right of the big window, was an alcove that I knew led to a small sitting room with a TV and several bookcases.

The dresser with the mirror was clearly Renata's domain. Across the top of it were spread all the tools of the womanly arts—a hair brush, a jewelry box, a wig, and a tray full of lipsticks, eye shadows, powders, and other elements of witchcraft. The other dresser top was blank by comparison; it only held a set of keys, some spare change, and a large container for pills marked off by the days of the week.

I had gotten about that far in my visual survey of the room when I heard the gasp, a sharp intake of breath behind me to the right. I jerked around, simultaneously swinging the bat into position for action.

And saw Renata Chalmers.

She stood in the doorway of the guest bathroom, her deep brown eyes dilated in surprise. Her right hand was on a middle button of her green and white blouse, as though she'd stopped dead in the act of dressing. The pale pink of a lacy bra was just visible. Okay, I noticed; I couldn't help it.

For a long moment, with her eyes fixed on me, I felt like a butterfly mounted on a pin in somebody's collection. The room was hot and my mouth was dry and this should have happened to somebody else, like maybe Ralph Pendergast.

"Jeff!" Renata said at last. Her eyes traveled down to the bat in my hand. "What are you doing in my room? And with that thing?"

I let my right hand and the bat drop to my side. "I thought I heard a noise," I said lamely.

"I pretty much always make a noise when I take a shower." The temperature of her voice was just this side of frigid. Her hair was damp from the steam of the shower and the Victorian ringlets from last night were gone. She buttoned her top two buttons as I avoided her eyes, certain that my face must be turning the color of her underwear.

"But there wasn't . . . there shouldn't have been anybody here," I stammered. "Mac left fifteen minutes ago. I was sure he would have taken everybody with him."

"He had to set up some things early," Renata said. "My husband and your sister did go along, but I wasn't ready yet. You could have knocked, you know."

"It's this murder business and the robbery, I guess. It has me on edge. I'm sorry. I feel ridiculous."

"You look it, too," she said. "A baseball bat, yet!"

She laughed and I managed a smile. "It was the nearest weapon I could grab to defend myself."

"Well, thanks for not using it on me. Are you going over to the colloquium or do you have more sleuthing to do?"

Both, actually. The colloquium is where I would see and interview the people on Mac's list. Without telling Renata that, I offered to give her a lift in my seldom-used 1998 Volkswagen New Beetle, but she demurred.

"On a morning like this I'd just as soon walk," she said. "It isn't that far."

True enough, so I decided to leave my bike at home and walk with her. It was still cooler outside than you'd expect from the brightness of the sun, but it was perfect for a brisk walk. The long-legged Renata, swinging her huge handbag, set a pace I had to work to keep up with.

"It's hard to believe Hugh's dead," she said. "He was so lively."

"Maybe too lively. He had quite a reputation for playing to win, no matter what the game."

She nodded. "The reputation was well deserved. And what you must have heard about his success with the ladies—that was true, too."

I let that pass. "Your husband and Matheson didn't get along, did they?"

"Well, you saw them yesterday."

"Yeah, and I've also heard stories."

"Probably true."

I shook my head and said I found it amazing that grown men could be so venomous over a shared hobby.

"There's a little more to it than that," Renata said.

"Meaning?"

She shook her head. "It doesn't matter now."

I supposed she was right. Chalmers was on Mac's list of people to suspect or at least interview, but Mac himself had provided the old man's alibi for the period when Matheson was murdered.

But there were other members of the Anglo-Indian Club on that list, people Renata would know.

"Tell me about Molly Crocker," I said.

"She's one smart cookie, Jeff—plus ambitious, aggressive, and tough. She was especially tough on deadbeat dads when she was a prosecutor. Her fans call her Maximum Molly."

"Are you one of her fans?"

"You could say that. I'm going to be the treasurer of her re-election campaign."

Bias noted.

"What were her relations with Matheson?" I asked.

"I have no reason to think that she had any outside of the club, other than the fact that she's female—which, come to think of it, is a pretty compelling reason. And I guess Hugh might have tried some cases in front of her. You ask a lot of question, Mr. Cody. Shades of Sherlock!"

"Now that hurts, Mrs. Chalmers. I'm not the Sherlockian here—you are."

She shook her head. "Not me, my husband. Don't get us confused. I have my own interests."

"Music and art and things cultural, right?"

"That's another question."

"I have more. For instance, is Noah Queensbury for real?"

"His wife must think—"

"I mean about Sherlock Holmes," I interrupted, impatient.

"He's a gifted surgeon. I suspect that he works hard and plays hard. That Holmesmania stuff is his way of playing. He may act crazy, but I think it's just an act."

I paused at an intersection, waiting for a WALK light. Renata, seeing no cars coming our way, jaywalked. I scampered to keep up.

"Were any of your friends, or just people you know from the colloquium, late for the banquet last night?"

She shrugged. "I wouldn't know. I got held up fixing my hair into those ringlets I wore last night."

We were within sight of Muckerheide Center now, the flat slabs of some architect's tribute to Frank Lloyd Wright rising above the horizon before us.

"But your husband was there as early as the cocktail hour," I pointed out. "Mac said so."

"Sure. When I saw how long it was going to take to fix my hair, I told him to go on without me. He and Kate and Mac were all dressed, and they're more social creatures than I am anyway. And even a husband and wife need a little personal space between them now and then, don't you think?"

Personal space . . . it sounded like an echo of Lynda's constant complaint that I was too clingy, too jealous, too bossy—and after a while, just too *too*. Maybe things between us never would have gone off the rails if I had lightened my touch a bit. Maybe that was still possible.

"I guess I'm not qualified to answer that one," I said. "I mean, I've never been married." Not that I was against the idea.

I glanced in her direction, trying not to look like a man looking at a woman. I'm sure I failed miserably. It was hard to get away from the fact that Renata Chalmers was a stunningly attractive and sensuous female married to a man about forty years older than she was. I'd have bet he felt no such craving for personal space.

Sunday, March 13

9:00 Breakfast (President's Dining Room)
Field Bazaar

Session Four

10:00 "Dr. John H. Watson: Conductor of
Light"—Dr. Noah Queensbury, BSI,
Cincinnati

10:30 "Holmes on the Radio"—Bob
Nakamora,Philadelphia

11:00 "Humor in the Canon"—Dr.
SebastianMcCabe, BSI, Erin, Ohio

11:30 Sherlockian Auction—Bob Nakamora

12:00 Farewells and Thanks
Certificate of Participation

Chapter Twenty-Four
Bacon, Eggs, and Suspicion

I took my leave of Renata at the registration table outside the Hearth Room. She continued on to the President's Dining Room, although we were too early for breakfast, while I lingered to talk with Popcorn.

My administrative assistant, four feet eleven inches of romantic imagination wrapped up in a grandmother of three, was still swept up in *Love's Savage Desire*.

"Is this your first time through that book or are you re-reading the steamy parts?" I asked, as if I didn't know the answer. In her opinion, I don't put enough sex and violence in my books. She's a widow.

Popcorn sighed and set down the paperback. "I saw Lynda earlier." She wasn't at church, then, at least not any more. "Are you two an item again?"

"I'm not sure," I said, "but keep an eye on her Facebook status."

Turning away from Popcorn's blue cat's eyes, I found myself looking at the coat rack next to the registration desk. There were only a couple of coats on it, and no hats at all. I strained to remember what it had looked like yesterday.

"Did you notice anybody taking a deerstalker off of that rack yesterday afternoon?" I asked Popcorn.

Anybody who had a thing like that at a program like this would most likely want to wear it all the time, like Queensbury, not warehouse it on a coat rack—unless maybe he was saving it up to wear as a sort of disguise during the commission of a murder.

But Popcorn shook her head. "I don't think so. I couldn't swear to it because I was taking money and handing out name tags when I wasn't reading my book, but I don't think so. Why, is there one missing?"

"Probably not. It was just a thought."

I left Popcorn to her book, planning to join the breakfast crowd in the President's Dining Room. Before I got very far in that direction, though, I saw the bald-headed bookseller go in the second door of the Hearth Room with a box under his arm. Reuben Pinkwater, Mac had said his name was, and he was on Mac's list of people to interview.

I sidled up to him casually as he pulled books out of the box and stacked them on the long table. He was wearing gabardine pants, a small brown bow tie and white shirt with the sleeves rolled up. When he heard me coming he looked up and gave a cheery "Good morning."

The smile, showing off his gold tooth, put wrinkles in his face to match the soft indentions at the back of his head. It occurred to me then that all bald men over the age of thirty-five look alike, from Daddy Warbucks to Lex Luthor to Kojak.

But a deerstalker would hide a bald dome nicely.

"Morning," I agreed. "I haven't seen you around Erin." This was content-free chatter to get the ball rolling.

"Probably not. My shop's in Licking Falls. The Scene of the Crime. Here."

He handed me a business card with the name of the store and the unmistakable silhouette of Sherlock Holmes, the man in the deerstalker.

With the card in my hand I gestured to the small stack of deerstalker caps on one end of the table. "Do you sell many of those?"

He looked where I pointed. "A few a year. I thought I'd get rid of them all this weekend, but no such luck."

Pinkwater fussed with the books in jerky movements, squaring off volumes that already looked perfectly aligned to me. There were paperbacks and hardbacks of every size, some hot off the press and some barely held together with rubber bands. About ninety percent had either "Sherlock Holmes" or some obvious Sherlockian reference like "Baker Street" in the title.

"Isn't this kind of a narrow specialty?" I asked.

"Oh, I just brought the best of the Holmes stuff for this symposium or whatever it's called," he said. "We sell all kinds of mysteries. In fact, Al Kane's doing a book signing for us tomorrow night. See anything you like?"

Resisting the impulse to calculate the odds on that one, I said, "You have some old books here. There must be a few gems for collectors among them."

Pinkwater smiled. "Nothing that would excite a Woollcott Chalmers, that's for sure. I shy away from real rarities. You have to know what you're doing there or you can get burned. That happened to me once on a copy of *The Misadventures of Sherlock Holmes*, edited by Ellery Queen and very rare because it was suppressed by the Conan Doyle Estate. It turned out to be a modern bootleg reprint." He shook his head. "There's not much margin for that kind of error in this business."

What was that volume Pinkwater had showed me yesterday about a rare book that turned out to be fake? There it was, still on the table—*The Adventure of the Unique Hamlet.* There was the beginning of an idea there, if only I could put my finger on it.

"I never again bought a so-called rarity and I never will," Pinkwater concluded. "That's not the business I'm in."

"Never?"

"Never."

"But what if you did happen to acquire a book like that?" I pressed. "Say it just fell into your lap, something unique and worth thousands of dollars. Would you know where to resell it?"

"Sure." That smile again.

Now I was getting somewhere.

"Well, where?"

"Woollcott Chalmers. He'd buy it."

With a frustration bordering on despair, I thanked Mr. Clean and headed for the President's Dining Room in hopes of at least getting breakfast out of this deal. On the way I pulled out my notebook and struck a line through the names of Reuben Pinkwater and, now that I thought about it, Renata Chalmers.

For all of Mac's baloney about not having time to interview the people on his list, several shared his breakfast table—Judge Crocker, Dr. Queensbury, and Woollcott Chalmers. Kate and Renata were there, too, along with Al Kane, Bob Nakamora, and Lynda. *So there she was.*

As I joined them they were in the midst of an animated discussion that could only have concerned the late Hugh Matheson.

"He was a slickster, a trickster, and a damned womanizer," Chalmers said with a fire in his blue eyes, as if daring anyone to disagree.

Judge Crocker, seated immediately to Chalmers's left, concentrated on applying strawberry jam to a biscuit.

"Worst of all," Chalmers added, "he was a poseur. Most of what he knew about Sherlock Holmes he must have picked up from some old Basil Rathbone films. And the fact that he's dead doesn't change any of that."

"I fear that Hugh, rather like the victim in Agatha Christie's *Murder on the Orient Express*, had a more-than-ample share of detractors," Mac rumbled.

"Somebody must have liked him," Lynda said, "or he couldn't have been a womanizer."

She wore a short-sleeved yellow and blue dress with a bright floral design that was giving me spring fever. I tried not to give her too much eyeball time.

Mac paused from attacking his extremely unhealthful hash browns long enough to praise Lynda for clarity of reasoning "bordering on the Sherlockian." If she objected to his cheap flattery she didn't say so, but then she's always had a soft spot for Mac, regarding him for some mysterious reason as an adorable screwball.

"So who do you think killed Matheson?" Al Kane asked, directing the question at Chalmers.

"Perhaps some narrow-minded husband," the old collector said acidly.

"One who just happened to be wearing a deerstalker?" Mac said. "Come now, Woollcott, you ask us to believe too much."

"The way you talk about Matheson," Kane said to Chalmers, "are you sure you didn't do it yourself?"

Renata Chalmers sucked in her breath.

"Nonsense," her husband snapped. "Why would I do a horrible thing like that?"

It was hard to read the look behind Kane's rimless spectacles. He was either having a great time putting the old man on, or he was back to playing amateur sleuth and assigning Chalmers the role of villain.

"How about revenge?" Kane suggested. "That was a favorite motive of the late Sir Arthur Conan Doyle, if I recall correctly."

"Watson," Queensbury corrected under his breath.

Chalmers snorted. "Revenge for what? Revenge is for losers, not winners. If Matheson and I went after the same thing, I'm the one who inevitably walked off with it. Everyone knew that. I built a collection that Matheson would have paid a fortune to get his hands on, then I gave it away."

"Stop it—stop it, all of you!" Molly Crocker's voice was strained. Looking weary, she shoved strands of graying hair out of her eyes. "You're all playing fun and games with the death of a man most of us knew. As a jurist and a human being, I find that distasteful and unconscionable."

"I didn't know the victim," Bob Nakamora said, "but I think the lady's right."

"Indubitably," Mac concurred. "In letting our passion for sleuthing get the best of us, we have been insensitive louts." *Speak for yourself Mac; I wasn't in this for fun and games.*

"Maybe so," Queensbury said, "but the question remains: Whodunit? We all have a stake in the answer. You heard what Mac said earlier: A witness saw Hugh open his door to somebody wearing a deerstalker. Doesn't that make it look like one of us?"

In the awkward silence that followed, I wanted to point to the cap lying on the floor between his chair and Molly Crocker's and say, "You should know, Dr. Queensbury." But, of course, I politely restrained myself.

Then Bob Nakamora pointed out, "We still haven't solved the mystery of the stolen books. Maybe whoever took those books was also stealing something from Matheson, and Matheson caught him. Couldn't a clever burglar have noticed a lot of deerstalkers around the hotel and put one on so he'd fit in? They're not hard to buy."

Mac thumped the table. "Ingenious, Bob! But not, I fear, the truth. You see"—he knitted up his bushy eyebrows in concentration—"the killer demonstrably was not a burglar. A burglar is one who burgles something, a thief in the night, a cowardly creature of stealth. Not even a novice at that dishonorable craft knocks on his victim's door.

"Nor," Mac added, leaning forward, "would a man of law be likely to admit a stranger to his hotel room. The implication is clear: It was a friend or, at minimum, an acquaintance who killed Hugh Matheson."

That much I'd been sure of all along.

And now I was beginning to get a notion about why Matheson had had to die.

Chapter Twenty-Five
"I Think I'm on to Something"

After breakfast, while others drifted toward the Hearth Room for the first talk of the day, Mac followed me into the corridor

"You have something to report?"

"Not much. Just that I wouldn't put any money on Reuben Pinkwater for the killer if I were you." Only after I said it did I realize with bitterness the assumption Mac had made—that I would act the Watson (sorry, amanuensis) he expected me to be. "I don't even know why you want me talk to people on that damned list of yours," I added. "You could have interrogated most of them yourself right there at your breakfast table."

"I had no way of knowing that when I formulated the list," Mac said. "Of course, I did question my breakfast partners to a certain subtle degree before you arrived. However, I would still benefit from your objectivity as a total outsider and your considerable skills as an interviewer. And there are others—"

"All right, all right." When Mac refers to himself as subtle, it's time to shut him up. Besides, he was spreading on the butter awfully thick. "I've already talked to Pinkwater and Renata. I'll keep working my way down the list, unless I can prove the killer's identity before I get that far."

Mac paused with his hand halfway into his breast pocket. "You have been holding out on me, old boy. You have a theory."

"An idea, anyway. I think I'm on to something, but only an expert could tell me for sure. Who knows more about Sherlock Holmes first editions and stuff like that than anybody else here?"

"Woollcott," Mac said without hesitation.

"Aside from him."

Mac pulled a cigar from his pocket, for once without some hocus-pocus or even a dramatic flourish. "Lars Jenson. He can readily describe all five Croatian editions of some obscure Spanish pastiche. He is even adept at certifying the handwriting of several important Sherlockian figures. What are you groaning about, Jefferson?"

"The Swedish Chef. It would have to be him. Even if he tells me what I need to know I'll never be able to understand it."

"Admittedly, English is not his best language. He and I mostly communicate in German, sometimes Italian." *Show-off.*

I asked Mac to go with Jenson and me to the library as an interpreter, but he shook his head and said it was impossible. In a few minutes he had to acknowledge the tragic death of Hugh Matheson and say a few appropriately kind words. He was also scheduled to introduce Dr. Queensbury's talk on "Dr. John H. Watson: Conductor of Light" and Bob Nakamora's on "Sherlock Holmes on Radio," then speak himself on "Humor in the Canon." He dared not risk Queensbury or Nakamora coming up short and leaving the audience at a loss for a host, as had happened on one embarrassing occasion already. *What, Sebastian McCabe couldn't bi-locate?*

"However," Mac said, "I would be delighted to use my good offices to persuade Lars to accompany you, should such persuasion prove necessary. Of course"—he cocked an eyebrow as he gestured airily with the unlit cigar—"that would be all the easier if I knew what the bloody hell you have in mind, Jefferson."

"Are you ready to explain your mumbo-jumbo about Matheson not being the thief? No? I didn't think so. Well, this time I'm the detective and I get to do mysterious things without explaining."

Besides, if I told him my idea and it proved wrong, I'd look like the biggest fool outside of Congress.

Mac took my reticence in good humor, promising to pull Jenson out of the Hearth Room where he was awaiting the start of the program. With an aggressive lope, he crossed the hallway and disappeared into the Hearth Room. As I was watching him go, Lynda blindsided me on my right.

"Okay, Jeff," she said. The greeting, totally unexpected and out of context, made me jump slightly. "You two had your Boys' Night Out. Now, what gives?"

"You!" I said, investing the syllable with the most accusatory tone I could muster. "You sure didn't do me any favors with those two stories in the paper this morning."

"I'm sorry, Jeff, I really am, but doing you favors isn't part of my job description at the *Observer*. You never seem to get that." She ran a hand through her honey-colored hair, a nervous gesture.

"Any more of this crap and I'm going to lose *my* job. I wish you could have at least quoted Ralph in the—oh, never mind."

I was overcome by the depressing familiarity of a scene played out so many times before. The conflict between Lynda's job and mine had been a constant irritant the whole time we had dated. Here it was again, just when I was hoping that what we had been through together yesterday, and the conspiracy of silence about it that still bound us together, meant that our romantic relationship was no longer in the dead letter file. And even before that, she had said she loved me—and then called me an idiot. Confused as well as depressed, I changed the subject.

"I didn't expect to see you here this morning," I said.

"It seemed the place to be. This is where the murderer is." She gripped her purse with a force that turned her knuckles white. "Look, Jeff, I want to know if you and Mac have any idea who killed Matheson—because Oscar and his crew don't. They may never find those books in his room if they aren't even looking for them. And that means they won't know Matheson was the thief, which could turn out to be the biggest clue of all. I think we screwed up last night by not calling 911 and telling the whole story as soon as we found the body. It would have been a lot easier on my nerves."

"Not if you were in jail."

She ignored that. "Unless you have any better ideas, it's not too late to tell Oscar about the books."

"Somebody in housekeeping at the hotel will find the books eventually. Besides, Matheson didn't steal them."

"What?"

"That's what Mac said, and I have to admit that he's right often enough that the other times don't count."

Lynda yanked open her purse, pulled out a stick of gum, unwrapped it, and shoved it into her mouth. "If he wasn't the thief, then why did he have the books?"

"Mac wouldn't tell me that much. He's acting mysterious about it. But it could be that Matheson actually *recovered* the books somehow, only for some reason didn't find all of them. Anyway, what's really important is, I have an idea that may explain why Matheson died, if not who—"

I stalled out when I saw Mac coming out of the Hearth Room with Lars Jenson.

"Jefferson," my brother-in-law called. "Lars is quite amenable to assisting you. Have you met?"

We hadn't, although I had watched the tall, stooped Swede in the library. Mac introduced him to Lynda and me.

"A great pleasure," Jenson said in that sing-song voice. He bowed at Lynda, oh-so-Continental and old-fashioned. She stuck out her hand for shaking. After a while Jenson figured out what he was supposed to do with the hand, and he did it. Then he turned to me. "You like to look at some books now, *ja*?"

"*Ja*," I said.

"And Lynda makes three," she added.

You may think we'd have trouble getting into the Lee J. Bennish Memorial Library on a Sunday during spring break, and normally you'd be right. But things weren't normal. Guards were all over the place, inside and out. The Campus Security people knew me. And even if they hadn't, my staff ID card would have been at a high enough level to get me past them.

Gene Pfannenstiel's office, full of ancient books spilling out of bookcases, looked almost Dickensian except for the laptop computer open on his roll-top desk. The gnome looked up from it in surprise when we entered.

"Oh, hi," he said. "What are you folks doing here? It's Sunday, isn't it?"

"Yeah," I said, "but we have a distinguished visitor all the way from Sweden and we wanted to take him on a quick tour of the Chalmers Collection."

Jenson smiled. "*Ja, ja.*"

Gene regarded Jenson shrewdly. "Didn't I see you yesterday during—"

"We'll only be a few minutes," Lynda interrupted. "He can't stay long."

"Right," Gene said, reaching down to tie a lace on his right gym shoe. "I'm knee-deep in cataloguing right now, but go ahead and look. The guards won't stop you. They'll just watch you real closely if you touch any books."

"Actually, that might happen," I said. "Dr. Jenson is a serious scholar. Can you unlock the cases where the best stuff is on display?"

He agreed without complaint.

While we were walking from his office to the rare book room, where the Chalmers Collection was on display, I asked Gene whether he'd heard anything from Decker about the books that were stolen.

"Nothing, I'm afraid."

"Did you know Hugh Matheson, the man who was murdered?" I didn't expect an affirmative answer, and I didn't get one.

Gene shook his head. "That was a terrible thing, wasn't it? The murder. No, I didn't know him, but I must have seen him if he was at the library yesterday, huh? I saw so many people."

I tried to think of more questions Mac might ask, since Gene was on his infamous little list, but I drew a blank. So did Lynda.

When we reached the Chalmers Collection, I could practically hear Larsen's pulse race faster as he shoved his glasses against his nose and bent down to read the titles in the foreign section. He talked to himself in Swedish as he pulled out a book called *Sherlock Holmes aventyr*.

I tugged on his sleeve and led him to where Gene was unlocking the cases holding the rarest remaining gems of the Chalmers Collection.

"Mr. Jenson," I said, "I want you to look at as many of these books as you can with extreme care and tell me if each of them is exactly what it's supposed to be. Are the first editions really first editions and are any inscriptions inside genuine? Understand?"

"*Ja.* Just like a mystery. I am sleuth."

Gene's eyes widened. "It's just a wild idea," I assured him. "There's probably nothing to it. Relax. Go back to your cataloguing. The guards will keep an eye on us." I wanted him gone. He was a suspect.

"Okay. Call me if you need me."

When Gene was out of earshot, Lynda said, "That's your brilliant idea?" Her tone lacked the admiration I would have hoped for. "You think the books in the Chalmers Collection might be fakes?"

"I didn't say it was brilliant; I said it could explain why Matheson was murdered. I got the idea from a Sherlock Holmes story that was described to me. It's about a collector who steals his own book to keep a rival from finding out that it's a phony. Now maybe somebody killed Matheson for the same reason—because when he got his hands on those missing books they turned out to be frauds. And if that's true, other books in the Chalmers Collection could be just as spurious."

"But that would mean that Chalmers himself is the killer," Lynda said.

Jenson murmured over a faded red volume.

I shook my head. "That's where truth has to depart from fiction. Chalmers never would have donated fraudulent books to begin with. He'd know that at the college they'd be available to scholars who could expose them."

"Then if the Chalmers Collection was the real stuff when it got here, parts of it must have been stolen and replaced later," Lynda said. "That little librarian must have done it, or at least been involved."

"Yeah," I said miserably. "Gene wouldn't be the first academic librarian who peddled rare books, as Queensbury reminded me yesterday. I don't want to believe it, but that's where my logic leads me."

"Well, I'm not sure your logic is so logical. If your scenario is correct, then the two books we found in Matheson's room must be phonies. Why would the killer leave those behind where somebody else could see the fakery?"

"Because the killer couldn't find them—he wasn't as clever at searching as you were. The other book, the one that's still missing, was hidden somewhere else and he found that one."

She took a wad of gum out of her mouth and wrapped it in foil. "Back up a minute, Jeff. How could Matheson spot these books for phonies? He was no expert on Sherlockiana. He was a guy with a collection and a lot of bucks to spend on it."

"That's what Chalmers said—talking about his bitter rival. We don't know whether that's true or he was just dissing the competition."

I think I had her there, because she said, "All right, then, this gets me back to where I was before: The cops need to know that Matheson had those books."

Before I had a chance to answer, Jenson poked his soulful gray eyes up over the book in his hands. *Three Problems for Solar Pons*, the title read. What in the world could that be?

"Excuse me please," the Swede said. "Your theory is most intriguing, Jefferson,"—Yefferson—"but I do not believe it is so very likely."

"Why not?" I demanded.

"You expect lots of fakes, *ja*? Not the missing books only." He shook his head vigorously. "I have look at ten, fifteen books here. I find no fakes."

Chapter Twenty-Six
I've Got Your Number

Outside the library, in the fresh air of a beautiful spring Sunday, I pulled out my notebook.

"Now what?" Lynda said.

"Just crossing names off Mac's list."

When the truth hits you in the face, there's no point in trying to smack back. I didn't kid myself that there were another ten or fifteen phony books that Jenson had missed.

"Don't be too hard on yourself, Jeff. It wasn't a bad idea, really."

"I know. In fact, it was as swell idea. I'm going to write it down and use it in a Max Cutter story."

I flipped through the notebook, looking for a blank page, until I saw something that brought me back from the fictional world of my Philadelphia private eye with a jerk.

"What are you staring at?" Lynda asked. It's that journalistic DNA of hers; she's always full of questions.

"Something I'd forgotten all about," I told her.

I showed her a page containing nothing but three digits—525. It was the number I'd copied off the notepad in Matheson's room, presumably a hotel room number that the lawyer had called or intended to call the day he died.

Jenson looked on with a mixture of interest and puzzlement, clearly curious but too polite to ask what was going on. When we reached the Hearth Room we shook hands with him again, thanked him, and let him get back to the lunacy at hand.

I pulled out my phone, tapped on the number for the Winfield from my contacts list, and asked for room 525.

Five rings, six rings, seven . . .

What are there, ten rings to a minute? I'd given up counting by the time a generic hotel voicemail message kicked in. I disconnected in disgust.

"We should have expected that, you know," Lynda said. "Whoever has that room isn't going to be just sitting around waiting for us to call. He's going to be in there." She pointed at the Hearth Room across the way. "I mean, it's got to be one of the Sherlockians. Unless Graham Bentley Post—"

"No, it's not his room number."

Although the popular culture maven was staying at the Winfield, I had a clear recollection that the room number he'd written on his business card began with a seven. I pulled it out of my wallet for a quick confirmation: room 718.

"I bet the hotel won't tell us who's in that room if we just call them out of nowhere," Lynda said, "but there must be some way to find out."

"Yeah. Mac would find a way."

I cracked open the door at the front of the Hearth Room about four inches. Noah Queensbury was talking but with the air of a man winding down, while Mac looked on benignly from his throne-like chair across the room. I opened the door wider and signaled my brother-in-law with all the agitated movement of a spasmodic semaphore operator. Finally I caught his eye and he caught my meaning. He shook his head no. I shook my head yes. Glowering, he stalked behind Queensbury and over to the door.

"Jefferson," he said heavily, "eager as I am for another progress report, this is a most infelicitous time. Couldn't you tell me about your adventures after the Sherlockian auction?"

"Fine, fine." For what I had to report so far, I was in no hurry. "But we need some help right now."

"We're trying to learn the occupant of a certain room at the Winfield," Lynda said. "It's probably one of your colloquium people. Can you help us put a name to the number?"

"Of what possible interest—"

"I thought you were in a hurry," I said. This was my show, and this time Mac was *my* assistant.

The sound of applause came from inside the Hearth Room, magnified by the speakers in the corridor. Mac looked toward the room and tugged at his beard. "Blast it, nobody ever did this to Nero Wolfe! I do not have access to the colloquium participants' room numbers. You will have to call Sandy Roeder at the Winfield and ask her who is registered for that room. Mention my name. Sandy is a former student of mine."

"R-O-E-D-E-R?" Lynda asked. "Doesn't she own the Winfield?"

"Not yet. Her mother has that distinction. You shall owe me dearly for this."

Without further farewell, he slipped back into the Hearth Room (if an elephant can slip).

"He means he was happy to be of help," I told Lynda, who was already pulling out her Android.

Sandy Roeder wasn't an easy sell. I could tell that from Lynda's hand gestures, and never mind what they were. But finally she disconnected and stuck the phone back in her purse with a satisfied look on her face.

"I'm not going to try to guess," I told her, "so just give. Whose room is it?"

"Molly Crocker."

Chapter Twenty-Seven
Here Comes the Judge

I don't know that I expected to hear, but not that.

"Molly Crocker doesn't seem like his type, does she?" Lynda said, noting the shock on my face.

"Come to think of it," I said, "why not? She's female." In fact, she was an attractive, albeit mature, female. "She's married, but that wouldn't even slow Matheson down, much less stop him. There must have been some sort of relationship between them—her room number on the writing pad shows that—and romance is certainly one of the possibilities."

"Certainly. I withdraw what I said about his type. How would I even know, really?"

"And maybe she went to his room at the Winfield yesterday with her hair tucked up in a deerstalker cap. Somebody who saw her from behind might not have been able to tell she was a woman. In fact, now that I think about it, are we sure the witness said anything about gender? I think Oscar used the pronoun 'he,' but maybe he was just making an assumption. We should press him on that."

"But Crocker was wearing a dress every time I saw her yesterday," Lynda objected.

She stopped talking as a female student walked by, one of the lost souls from the dorm who hadn't gone home for spring break. The girl was tall with platinum blond hair reaching down the middle of her back. She wore very short red shorts (at least two months ahead of season) over long, muscular legs, a white T-shirt with no bra underneath, and Nike gym shoes. I barely noticed her.

"Besides," Lynda said when the student had passed, "what about motive? What do you figure Molly Crocker had to do with the stolen books?"

"I don't know, maybe nothing at all. This could be a simple crime of passion. It could have been her, not you, that Matheson referred to when he told Queensbury he had business with a lady. We ought to at least talk to her, find out if she knows anything. Her name is on my list from Mac anyway."

Lynda had to admit it couldn't hurt.

I went into the back of the Hearth Room, where Bob Nakamora was now holding forth on the subject of Sherlock Holmes on the radio.

"Orson Welles played Holmes in his own radio adaptation of William Gillette's famous melodrama *Sherlock Holmes* when *The Mercury Theater on the Air . . .*"

After looking around for a minute from the doorway, I spotted Judge Crocker sitting next to Queensbury on a comfortable couch along the far wall. Even in the harsh fluorescent light of the Hearth Room she was a handsome woman. The blue jumper she was wearing seemed casual, comfortable and un-judgelike. Once again I noticed the mound of her tummy, big enough to make me wonder if she were pregnant but not big enough that I'd risk asking her about it.

Feeling conspicuous, I crossed the room and whispered in her ear. "Could you come with me for a minute?"

Molly Crocker looked at me, then at Queensbury, who seemed engrossed in the talk. She rose and picked up her purse, a dark leather contraption with a drawstring top. Not until we were walking toward the door did she speak in a low voice.

"Has something happened?"

There were a million ways to answer that. I settled on, "Nothing new. We just want to ask you a few questions."

"We?"

The presence of Lynda Teal right outside the door answered for me. Molly had met Lynda at breakfast, and apparently she thought I'd set her up for an exercise in ambush journalism.

"If you want to talk to me about Hugh's death,I must tell you that I have no interest in being interviewed for your newspaper," she told Lynda.

"I'm really the one who wants to talk to you," I said. "Off the record. You could help us solve Matheson's murder."

"Mr. Cody, I think I made it quite clear earlier this morning that I highly disapprove of playing games with murder."

"This is no game."

"Then if you actually have any pertinent information about this homicide or any other crime you're legally bound to tell the police."

"So are you."

"What's that supposed to mean?" Her tone of voice would have cut through diamonds.

While I was making a mental note to never do anything that might land me in Maximum Molly's courtroom, the girl in red shorts walked by again. "I don't think the hallway is the right place to discuss this," I said.

After a token protest that there was no right place, Molly went with us to the Study Lounge on the same floor of Muckerheide. With its stuffed chairs and fifty-watt bulbs, the place is about as conducive to study as the drive-in theaters of my father's youth, and occasionally is the site of similar activities. Not today, though. We had the lounge all to ourselves, thanks to spring break.

As soon as we'd settled into chairs I told Molly, "The number of your room at the Winfield was written on a notepad by the side of Matheson's body."

"Good grief, is that what this is about? I already know that. Your police chief—what's his name, Hummel?—he told me this morning."

Lynda, sitting where Molly Crocker couldn't see it, rolled her eyes in the back of her head.

"Oscar talked to you as part of his investigation?" I asked Molly.

"Yes. I found him a rather unpolished personality."

That was Oscar, all right.

I should have expected this. We'd left the notepad where we'd found it, like good citizens. Any idiot would have tried to find out whose number that was, and Oscar is no idiot. He just acts like it sometimes.

"Do you have any idea why Matheson had your number?" Lynda asked.

The judge turned to her. "I know exactly why, but I see no reason to tell you—on or off the record. As an officer of the court I've already told the proper authorities."

"It's really not that hard to figure out," I said. "Matheson was a notorious womanizer. That's an old-fashioned word that Chalmers used, but I don't know of a better one. The two of you must have had a liaison at the hotel. The only real question is whether you left his room before or after the murder."

Molly stood up, her body trembling. "That accusation is totally baseless."

Fortunately, I wasn't within slapping range.

"Jeff isn't accusing you of anything," Lynda said in a soothing tone. "He just got carried away for a minute. What he means is, did you go to Matheson's room yesterday afternoon? And if you did, did he give you any indication that he was expecting another visitor?"

"Those are questions quite proper for the police to ask, Ms. Teal, and they already did."

I gave up. "If you choose to stonewall us, Judge, I know there's nothing we can do about it. Legally, whatever you had going with the victim is none of our business."

"I had nothing 'going' with Hugh Matheson."

Unexpectedly, she sat back down and went on in a more collected voice. "I've known Hugh for years, since law school. Apparently he tried to call me at the hotel a couple of times Friday night, but I was at Mac's party. Anyway, on Saturday he missed me again because I was out to an early breakfast, so he followed me into the corridor after Kate McCabe's presentation."

"He just wanted to talk to you?" I said.

She nodded. "It was about a case he was involved in, a case that's going to reach my court."

"But that isn't ethical, is it?" Lynda objected.

"Totally inappropriate," the judge agreed with a shake of her head. "I told Hugh in the strongest terms possible that it was only our long friendship that kept me from reporting him to the ethics committee of the Cincinnati Bar Association."

It was as neat an explanation for an embarrassing circumstance as I'd ever seen, maybe too neat.

"I find it hard to believe that a man with a five-speed libido like Matheson could resist putting the moves on an attractive woman like you," I told Molly.

She laughed. "Thanks, I guess, but I never said he didn't try. I turned him down years ago, before I even had my first gray hair. I wasn't interested in being added to his list of conquests. And these days he prefers—preferred—younger women, so I was safe from his attentions."

Lynda must have read something significant in that—is that a woman thing?—because she said, "How young?"

"How young is Renata Chalmers?"

It took a second or two for that to penetrate. But when it did, it hit hard. I gripped the arm of my chair. "Are you telling us that Renata and Matheson—"

Molly Crocker rose to her feet, looking away from me as I stood up at the same time. "I'm sorry. I've already said far more than I had any business saying."

"Maybe so, but you did say it," Lynda pointed out, leaving her chair as well. "Now you at least have a responsibility to make sure we don't misinterpret and imagine the situation as any worse than it is."

"The situation is bad enough," the judge said, "at least by my rather traditional standards of morality. I really don't feel comfortable talking about it."

Talk about shutting the barn door after the cow's escaped . . .

"We're not gossips or voyeurs looking for cheap thrills," Lynda said. "We're asking for a reason. This could have a bearing on the murder motive."

"I—I never thought—"

I pressed the issue hard. "Was Renata Chalmers having an affair with Hugh Matheson or wasn't she?"

Molly closed her eyes. "Yes. Yes, damn it, she was."

"How do you know?"

"I had the ill-fortune to wander into the bar just before a meeting of the Anglo-Indian Club some months ago. Hugh and Woollcott were in there, arguing so intently they didn't notice anyone else. It was an ugly scene—Hugh bragging that he'd been bedding Woollcott's wife right under his nose for six months. He was like . . . like some hunter holding up a prize catch."

"Or maybe a collector who'd bested a rival," I murmured.

"The whole thing was so dehumanizing that I only wanted to run out of there and forget about it. I turned around and bumped smack into Renata. She'd heard it all; I could tell by the look on her face."

"So her husband knew and she knew that he knew," Lynda said.

I hadn't observed any great strain between the Chalmerses and I said so.

"Woollcott is nothing if not a pragmatist," the judge said. "I suspect he could tolerate the situation as long as he maintained bragging rights in public. Renata is the perfect trophy wife, isn't she? Beautiful, talented, and intelligent. And her last name is Chalmers. Woollcott wasn't going to give that up over a little infidelity."

The delivery was so dry and factual that I couldn't tell if she were being catty or not. But it was just the sort of thing a jealous and envious woman might say.

"Just for the sake of discussion, Judge," I said, "where were you around the time of the murder—say an hour in either direction?"

"I don't know because I don't know when the murder happened. I presume I was dressing in my hotel room, enjoying the cocktail hour or in transit between the two. At any rate I was with my husband the entire afternoon and evening."

"Your husband?" Lynda echoed.

Her obvious surprise—and mine, too—put a smile on Molly Crocker's face.

"You mean you sleuths didn't know? I'm married to Noah Queensbury."

Chapter Twenty-Eight
The Key to Everything

The Crocker-Queensbury connection still had me numb some minutes after the distaff side of that combo had returned to the Hearth Room.

"I knew she was married because I noticed her wedding ring yesterday," I told Lynda, leaning my rear end against the escalator, "but why didn't somebody tell me her husband was Queensbury?"

"Why should they?" Lynda demanded. "Is that supposed to be the most important thing about her—who her husband is?"

"Maybe not, but it could be important enough, and there was no way for me to know it. Even the hotel room was in the Crocker name."

"Well, it had to be in one name or the other."

There was no way to respond to that without digging myself into a deeper hole, so I changed the subject.

"If Maximum Molly is married to Queensbury, she could have been wearing his deerstalker last night," I said.

"Oh, yeah? When does he ever take it off? I bet he even wears it to bed. Jeff, whoever was wearing that hat could have easily bought it, borrowed it or brought it from home. She or he didn't have to be married to it."

"I vote against buying," I said. "If the deerstalker was a kind of minimal disguise, the killer would have thought of that earlier and wouldn't have had to buy it here at the colloquium."

"You're assuming premeditation?" Lynda asked.

I nodded. "The use of a gun smacks of planning. I know we have a concealed carry law in Ohio, but I can't see these Sherlockians packing heat to a quiet campus in Erin."

"Maybe not, but I know who might have." She paused to give the name the appropriate amount of drama. "Al Kane. He's always shooting guns on those TV commercials."

"But he doesn't have any possible motive!"

"Correction: He doesn't have any motive that we've found out about yet. Don't dismiss him as a suspect just because you like his sexist, adolescent—"

"Okay, this isn't getting us anywhere," I interrupted. "I'm not writing off anybody as a potential suspect. For instance, Molly Crocker still could have been fooling around with Matheson, even though she is married and three months pregnant."

Molly had offered that last bit of information unsolicited.

It was easy to see Renata Chalmers with her septuagenarian husband as easy pickings for a handsome, charismatic dude like Matheson. She knew his reputation, but I bet all of his other women did, too. So why should Molly Crocker be any less vulnerable than anyone else just because she was a judge and a tough cookie?

"An affair between Molly and Matheson would give Queensbury a hell of a murder motive," I said. "Maybe Dr. Q. had just caught on to what his wife was up to and that's what his argument with Matheson was really about—not some Sherlock Holmes silliness, as Queensbury claimed. And as you just pointed out, Queensbury's been wearing a deerstalker all weekend. Don't overlook the obvious."

Lynda shook her head. "You're spinning this out of whole cloth and your fiction writer's imagination. Crocker just gave Queensbury an alibi. I hardly think she'd be protective of him if he'd killed Matheson in a fit of jealousy.

Anyway, I believe the judge when she said there wasn't anything between her and Matheson. As a political figure she had too much to lose."

"Wait a minute. What do you mean? Politicians get caught with their pants down all the time."

"Sure, men do. But can you think of a single female governor, senator or U.S. Representative who had to resign because of a sex scandal?"

She had me there. Whether that proved anything was beside the point, because Lynda steamed on:

"You can cross both her and Queensbury off your suspect list. The key to everything, Jeff, is something else Crocker said—bragging rights."

She tore the gold wrapping off of a Werther's Original caramel and popped the candy into her mouth.

"Remember how Crocker said she thought Chalmers could live with his wife's infidelity as long as he maintained bragging rights to her?" Lynda continued. "Well, how long do you think that would last? According to Crocker's account, Matheson was taunting Chalmers with the knowledge that he'd made time with Renata. That was probably the whole point of the affair for him—to take away, in a sense, another one of Chalmers's prize collectibles."

"I had that same feeling."

"Then do you suppose Matheson could be content to tell only Chalmers about it?" She shook her head. "No way. That was just the first step in humiliating the old man. Next he would have spread the word all around, making Chalmers a laughingstock, a comic opera cuckold."

"Chalmers wouldn't put up with that."

Lynda nodded. "That's my point."

"No, no, Chalmers as killer doesn't work. He couldn't have gone to the Winfield. Mac was with him during the murder hour, remember?"

"But at a cocktail party. You know how packed those things get and how time flies when you're talking and drinking, especially drinking. Chalmers could have slipped out for a half hour or forty-five minutes without Mac being any the wiser."

And Renata wouldn't have seen it, I thought. She'd been back at Mac's house, still fixing her hair in that elaborate 'do.

"He must have taken a cab to the Winfield," Lynda said with building excitement. "We can check that out easily enough through the cab company, or at least Oscar's troops could. Matheson's unknown visitor wore a deerstalker cap. How many of those do you suppose Chalmers owns?"

"About enough to outfit the Chinese army, I guess."

With a sense of exhilaration I was beginning to believe Lynda could be close to the truth, a truth Mac probably didn't suspect even though he had put Chalmers on the list to be interviewed.

"And what about Chalmers's precious stolen books?" I said.

"I don't know why he missed two of them, but I bet he has the one that's still missing. We need to search his room at the McCabes' house."

"I didn't see anything when I was there with Renata this morning."

Lynda's eyes dilated. "What were you doing—"

"I wasn't looking for the books," I said. *Wait, that didn't sound right.* "I'll explain later. I guess it would take a really thorough search to find the books if they were hidden, and I can't do that now. I have to take Nakamora to a live interview on WIJC in"—I looked at my watch—"five minutes."

"Fine. I'll do it."

Applause echoed over the speaker in the hallway. Bob Nakamora apparently had finished enlightening his audience about "Holmes on the Radio."

"You can't just go barging into Mac's house," I told Lynda.

"Why not? You would if you weren't tied up."

"I'm kin."

"And don't tell me you'll do it later," she said, talking right over me. She pulled a folded-up copy of the colloquium schedule out of her purse. "This is the perfect time because Mac's talking next. You can bet your sister and both Chalmerses will be hanging on every word. Nobody's going to go back to the house for anything."

All of a sudden we had a lot of company in the hallway. People were oozing out of the Hearth Room, taking advantage of the end of Bob Nakamora's talk to run outside for a smoke, hit the john, or just stretch their legs.

Nakamora himself paused just outside the doorway, straining his neck to look around. Renata Chalmers, standing next to him, tapped him on the arm and pointed at me. He smiled in relief and started coming my way.

"You win, dammit." I pulled the key to the McCabe household out of my pocket and gave it to Lynda. "Wipe your feet on the hall carpet before you go in."

"I always do. Meet you back here."

She snatched the key out of my hand like one of those toy banks that grabs your coins. She was down the escalator by the time Bob Nakamora reached me.

"Are we going to be late for the interview?" he fretted.

"Not if we hurry. Come on."

As we descended on the escalator, Renata Chalmers peered over the railing at us, her lovely face devoid of any expression that I could read. What did she know about the murder, I wondered, and what did she suspect?

We reached the main level and kept going down. The studios of WIJC-FM, like the offices of the campus newspaper, *The Spectator*, are located on the lower level of Muckerheide Center. *The Spectator* was shut down for spring break, but not the radio station, which is college-owned but not exclusively student-run. With impeccable timing, Tony Lampwicke was just finishing his interview with the author of some incredibly obscure (and therefore noteworthy) academic book when we arrived.

The long-time host of the weekly *Crosscurrents* program nodded to acknowledge our presence and moved smoothly into an introduction of a new topic in his heavy British accent. "Very stimulating indeed," he said to an invisible conversation partner, apparently a telephone interviewee. "I'm sure your fine book will spark quite a revival of interest in Bulgarian neoclassicism. You know, the medium of radio itself is undergoing something of a revival these days . . ."

Lampwicke famously has a penchant for analyzing everything beyond the bounds of reason with a humorless intensity. He must be well into his forties, but he somehow seemed younger sitting behind the microphone in his loafers and cable knit sweater. His chin was sharp enough to be a lethal weapon and was covered by a neatly trimmed goatee.

"We have with us in the studio today on *Crosscurrents* an expert on old-time radio, and particularly the many radio adventures of Sherlock Holmes, the famous . . ."

I wanted to pace or crack my knuckles or do anything other than sit and listen to those two babble on. Most of all I wanted to join Lynda at Mac's house. Finally, I couldn't stand it anymore and I eased myself out of the studio. After all, I'd done my duty just by making sure that Nakamora had arrived on time. I was sure he could find his way back upstairs.

The glass door to the studio had just closed behind me when I heard, "Cody! Hold it right there."

It was the law. And he was wearing a deerstalker cap.

Chapter Twenty-Nine
Police Procedures

"Popcorn told me I'd find you here."

"Oscar, you look ridiculous in that deerstalker," I said.

"I'm just trying it on." At least he had just enough taste to sound a little defensive. "You liked the Panama hat better?"

I ignored that.

We started walking toward a bench across from the studio.

"How's the investigation going?"

"It's continuing."

Wow, that was informative. "Throw me a bone here, Oscar. For instance, did you find out who it was your witness saw coming out of Matheson's room, wearing the deerstalker?" He hesitated, as if he didn't want to tell me, so I went into persuasion mode. "Come on, Oscar. I have a stake in this. We're on my turf here. I just want to know where things stand."

He shook his head. "Nobody admitted it, and it could have been just about any clown in this carnival."

We sat down.

"Including a woman?" I pressed. "You said 'he' when you told me about it, but couldn't it have been a woman, like Molly Crocker, for example?" I was having a hard time letting go of that particular bone, even though I liked her.

"I guess so, if she were dressed in a man's clothing or something that could pass for it—gender-neutral, I guess you'd call it. Funny you should mention the judge, though. We had an interesting conversation, for reasons I won't get into. I think she's clean. If she hasn't killed that lunatic she's married to, I figure she wouldn't kill anybody."

I could see his point. That would make an interesting defense strategy.

"So you're nowhere on the deerstalkers?"

"I didn't say that and don't put words in my mouth. I got the names of the five people who bought deerstalkers from that guy selling them along with the books. I've got Gibbons working the list."

Damn. I should have pressed Pinkwater on that.

"Five not counting you, I presume. Anybody I know?"

"I don't know who you know, but I'm drawing the line there, pal. I'm not giving you any names. Besides, it may not mean anything anyway. We've got a new witness, a woman on the housekeeping staff, who got a better look at a guy coming out of Matheson's room."

Now he tells me. In the news business, that's what is known as "burying the lead."

"He was a redhead," Oscar added. "That's all I know right now. What I wanted to tell you is, I'm going back to the Winfield right now to interview the witness myself."

Somebody saw me. Fighting panic, I tried to pretend my hair wasn't the color of a carrot and this couldn't possibly have anything to do with me.

"Al Kane is a red-head," I mused, hating myself for casting suspicion on one of my favorite writers. "And we know he likes guns." I was thinking of all those years of National Pistol Association commercials that ended with him pointing a Magnum .357 right at the viewer.

"He claims he's never even owned a gun," Oscar said. "I've got a search warrant to have all the hotel rooms checked. We're looking for a .32 revolver. The bullet was still in the body, didn't go right through. That and the fact that there were no powder burns—'tattooing' they call it—probably means the killer wasn't too close to the body. Now, that's kind of odd. How far away can you get in a hotel room? But it doesn't tell us much. And, of course, the killer wiped the place clean of fingerprints."

Happy as I was that I hadn't missed any of my prints or Lynda's, I also felt guilty that I'd possibly destroyed important evidence. But what were the chances of that, really? In detective stories, fingerprints are almost always false clues that get the wrong people in trouble. Surely whoever killed Matheson knew enough to wipe up afterwards.

"But I have a hard time figuring Al Kane for this," Oscar went on. "From what I can tell, he's about the least popular guy here but that's just because he isn't one of those Sherlockian wackos. I don't see a motive. In fact, I don't see a reason for anybody to kill Matheson. But then again, I also don't see why a guy with all his dough would steal the stuff from that collection. Kleptomania, maybe?"

"What!"

Oscar looked puzzled. "Didn't Ed Decker tell you? I told my guys to let him know. We found two of the missing books in Matheson's hotel room."

Chapter Thirty
Not Tonight, I Have a Headache

My surprise was a put-on, of course. Oscar's force is small but not incompetent. I knew they would find the books sooner or later, or the housekeeping staff would.

But Oscar wasn't within a mile of solving this murder. And so far as I could tell, neither was Mac—never mind his mysterious pronouncements designed to give that impression.

That left it up to me—and Lynda. Having no more real questions for the chief, I wrapped up the conversation and walked out of Muckerheide Center as casually as I could muster.

Then I broke into a jog.

Not much more than fifteen minutes later, taking a few shortcuts along the way, I arrived at the old McCabe house on Half Moon Street. I didn't have my key, having given it to Lynda, so I banged the iron door knocker. A long minute passed without the door opening. I banged again, loud enough to wake the dead. Still no answer.

Finally I turned the doorknob and gave an experimental push. The door opened.

"Anybody home?" I yelled, standing in the hallway. The words seemed to echo off the brass hall tree, the antique secretary, the framed paintings. Everything was familiar, yet somehow ominous. The silence was creeping me out. "Lynda!" I called

No response.

She might have completed her reconnaissance mission in Mac's guest suite and returned to St. Benignus already—except that I'd seen her yellow Mustang in the driveway outside my carriage house apartment.

I moved through the house slowly, like a thief in the night. That made no sense at all after the racket I'd already made, but I was functioning on the level of raw nerves and instinct now; sense or nonsense had nothing to do with it.

Within several feet of the guest suite I could see that the door was open. Nothing surprising about that, but it made the hair on the nape of my neck do handstands. I walked even slower, trying to prepare myself for whatever I might find in the room.

It didn't work, of course; nothing could prepare me for the awful sight of Lynda lying just inside the guest room, limp and lifeless as a marionette with its strings cut. Her body was curled almost in a fetal position, with her legs bent back and one of her blue-gray shoes off.

Unsteady on my legs, I dropped to my knees and felt her pulse. It was strong.

Satisfied that she was in no danger of dying, I held her hand and kissed her on the forehead. "Lynda, Lynda," I murmured, not expecting her to hear. "If we could get back together, I'd never be a jerk again."

Her eyelashes flickered. Her lips parted and a sound came out, halfway between a moan and a mumble.

"Lynda! Easy now," I said. "Don't strain yourself, honey."

She muttered something. I put my left ear next to her lips.

"Jeff." She swallowed.

"Yes?"

"What you just said. Was that a promise?"

"Well, I could try."

She managed a rueful grin. "Nice loophole. Listen, Jeff,I want you to know that Maggie didn't really break her ankle in a parachuting accident. She barely strained it."

"What?" This was so out of left field I wondered if she were delirious. "What are you talking about?"

"I'm fessing up. I'm telling you that I ordered Maggie to stay home and nurse her ankle yesterday so I could assign myself to the story because I missed you. You're a bundle of neurotic ticks and only slightly less crazy than McCabe, but I missed you so much that I just had to see you again."

That was somewhat like being slapped with her hand, then kissed by her lips, but the overall effect put me in serious danger of levitating. I tried not to show it.

"Then why'd you get rid of my picture in your apartment?" I asked.

"I didn't. I just moved it to the dresser in my bedroom. Get that leer off your face." She winced. "*Mamma mia*, what a headache. It feels like—Oh! Oh, no!" With a look of wild panic on her face, she jerked her hand away from mine, pulled herself up from the floor, and stumbled to the bathroom. Immediately came the sickening sound of repeated vomiting. When Lynda emerged again she was pale, washed out. I put my arm around her.

"I actually used to like mysteries," she said. "After this weekend, I'm not sure I can read them anymore."

"You never liked mine."

"I never said that. They're really pretty good, except for all that macho crap and the sexism."

Fighting the urge to respond to that, I said, "What the hell happened here?"

"I was in that other little room, the sitting room with the bookcases, when I thought I heard a sound in here. The room looked empty, but when I went on to check out the hallway I got conked from behind."

"The bastard must have been hiding in the bathroom. Let me look at your head."

Gently as I could I separated the matted hair to get a look at the wound. It was a bloody bump about the size of a quarter. I accidentally touched it with the tip of my index finger.

"Ow!" Lynda jerked away. "Sadist."

"It doesn't look too bad," I said, "but I understand that head wounds are tricky. You should go to the hospital."

"I should use dental floss and give up red meat, too. At least, that's what you used to tell me." She took a deep breath. "I don't want some doctor tapping my knee with his little mallet. Just give me a minute, I'll be okay."

"Whatever you say." *The new Jeff Cody is non-directional.* "Did you find anything while you were poking around?"

She shook her head, then winced. "No chance to. Why did somebody do this to me?"

"Because somebody wanted you out of the way before you could prove the identity of the killer."

"Chalmers?"

"I can't think of a better candidate. He looks frail, but maybe he hit you with his cane."

It didn't make sense that Chalmers would just leave her there, right in the place he was staying, but then maybe that's what we were supposed to think.

"The book," Lynda said suddenly, gripping my shoulder. "We still have to look for that missing Holmes book."

I talked her into letting me clean her wound first with soap and water and peroxide from the bathroom cabinet.

"As you said, this is where the killer had to be hiding," she pointed out as we stood in the bathroom. "We might as well start our search here."

I couldn't see hiding a priceless book in a room where people were taking showers and flushing the toilet.

Humidity is death on paper products. But we gave it a go. It wasn't an especially large bathroom, and a few minutes of intensive searching was enough to convince both of us that *Beeton's Christmas Annual* of 1887 wasn't hidden in the towels or wrapped in waterproof plastic inside the toilet bowl.

"Maybe it isn't hidden at all," I suggested. "Chalmers probably never dreamed anybody would be rude enough to search his rooms, not even his host's brother-in-law."

"And then maybe he didn't have time to hide it after he knocked me out," Lynda added. (Actually, that sounds pretty weak right now, but it didn't then.)

In the bedroom, she tackled Renata's dresser and I took Woollcott's—just the places a person might casually stick a book that wasn't much more than a fat pamphlet. I started my search with a once-over at the top of both dressers. His still had keys and coins and a bottle of pills, just as I'd seen that morning. Hers had all those womanly things like lipstick, a hair brush, a jewelry box, eye shadows, and powders.

And yet I had a nagging feeling that something was missing, something was not as it had been earlier that morning.

I opened a wine-colored bathrobe from the top drawer of Chalmers's dresser and unfolded it. No book hidden inside.

"How do you like this?"

I turned around to see Lynda holding up a red satin-and-lace nightie that clearly wouldn't hide anything.

"It's the real you," I assured her, my voice a little dry.

"You wish." She refolded the garment and put it back in Renata's drawer. "If the book was ever here it was probably removed while I was unconscious. Or maybe the whole idea that Chalmers killed—"

"Hold it."

I'd found something sandwiched between pairs of white undershorts. It was a little book with paper covers, about half an inch thick, five and a half inches wide and eight and a half long. There was a drawing on the cover in brown, a man lighting an old-fashioned lamp. Most of the printing was in black, including the part across the top where it said *Beeton's Christmas Annual.* But the title of the lead story, appropriately, was in big red letters—*A Study in Scarlet.* Gently, I turned to the first page and found a faded inscription in a handwriting I'd seen before:

> *Dear Ma'am,*
> *I hope this little detectivetale brings you some enjoyment.*
> *A.C.D.*

"This may be why you were hit on the head," I told Lynda. "To keep you from finding this."

Chapter Thirty-One
The Return of Sebastian McCabe

"It's the biggest story of my career," Lynda said as we drove back to Muckerheide Center in her Mustang, me at the wheel. "Murder, jealousy, sex, burglary, brilliant detective work—it has it all."

"Everything," I agreed, by no means happy.

I could imagine the headline stretched across the top of the *Observer* tomorrow—or the website today, for that matter. Even worse, I could see Ralph Pendergast's reaction to the news that the killer was Mac's house guest. Oh, this was going to get real ugly real fast.

Mac's talk on "Humor in the Canon" was over and a Sherlockian auction was underway by the time we arrived at Muckerheide Center. In fact, my elephantine brother-in-law was nowhere to be seen as we slipped into the seats at the back of the Hearth Room. The seat next to Kate was empty.

Sherlockian books and memorabilia donated by participants in the seminar were being sold to pay bills not covered by the modest registration fee and to build a kitty for next year's program, a highly optimistic presumption at this point. Some of the stuff on the block raised (or lowered) the word "obscure" to new levels. Tie tacks, greeting cards, mugs, Christmas ornaments, you name it— anything with a connection to Sherlock Holmes, no matter how tenuous, seemed to be fair game.

Bob Nakamora, acting as auctioneer, held up a volume about the size of a normal hardback book but with a faded red cover of paper. The illustration showed Holmes in his dressing gown.

"Here we have a rare edition of *The Incunabular Sherlock Holmes*," he announced. "There were only three hundred and fifty signed and numbered copies printed by the Baker Street Irregulars in 1958. This is number"—he opened the cover just a crack and peered inside—"ninety-four. What am I bid?"

Noah Queensbury, a couple of rows ahead of us, offered a dollar.

After some hesitation, a large woman in a print dress pushed it up to a dollar and a quarter.

"You may not have heard of this because it's so rare," Nakamora said, "but it was edited by the late, great Sherlockian Edgar W. Smith."

"Five dollars," Woollcott Chalmers said from across the room. He sat next to Renata, watching the auctioneer with eyes that betrayed an intensity of engagement. He cared what happened here.

"Six," Queensbury counter-bid.

"Ten." Chalmers's voice betrayed the ragged edge of irritation.

"What the hell's he coming on so strong for?" Lynda whispered. "He already owns every Holmes book known to humankind."

"Not anymore," I pointed out. "Besides, it's how you play the game that counts for somebody like him, and he plays the game to win."

Queensbury hung in until the bidding climbed up to twenty-five dollars, then flashed a nervous look at his spouse, the judge. Molly Crocker stirred in her seat. With obvious reluctance, Queensbury shook his head at Nakamora, silently taking himself out of the competition.

The smile on Chalmers's craggy face was a sort of victory flag as he limped up to claim his hard-won prize. He had plenty more to smile about in the next half-hour as a dozen or so other books piled up on Renata's lap.

"He must be trying to rebuild his whole blasted collection," Lynda said.

"Starting with that, I suppose," I said, nodding at the *Beeton's* concealed in a paper bag in Lynda's hand.

Just as the last item was sold (a *Hound of the Baskervilles* scarf that went to Barry Landers), Mac strode into the Hearth Room and up to the lectern. He removed the unlit cigar from his mouth as if to speak, but instead tossed the cigar into the air—where it turned into a yellow rose. He caught the flower and pinned it onto his boutonniere. Will the man never grow up?

"Weekends are always too short," he commented, "and this one has been shorter than most. Though marred by tragedy, this first annual 'Investigating Arthur Conan Doyle and Sherlock Holmes' colloquium has fulfilled all my hopes for a program that would be both entertaining and enlightening. What I mean is, it worked."

The crowd showed its agreement with applause—a little less thunderous than at other times during the weekend since maybe a third of the crowd had left early. Mac responded with a promise to reprise the program as long as they kept coming back.

"Until next time, then," he concluded, "I bid you farewell and beg you to remember: There's no police like Holmes!"

As he moved away from the lectern, he was mobbed by friends. Lynda and I finally cornered him a long five or ten minutes later. Being Mac, he acted like we'd been the ones missing in action.

"I need your report, Jefferson," he harrumphed.

"Where have you been while we were doing your legwork?" Lynda demanded.

"I was involved in legwork of my own, as it turned out," Mac said. "For one thing, I procured a verbal summary of the Sussex County coroner's findings."

"Oscar told me about that," I said. "There was a .32 revolver bullet still lodged in the body, no powder burns." Apparently shot from a distance, Oscar had said.

"Precisely, old boy! It makes the truth about the weapon transparent, does it not? Of course, the TV4 report was already highly suggestive in that matter."

"TV4?" I repeated. "What did the—"

"We can discuss that later. What did you find out from Gene Pfannenstiel? Molly Crocker? Renata and Woollcott? Noah Queensbury? Reuben Pinkwater?" He spit out the names like shots from a Tommy gun.

For all the talk *about* Queensbury, we hadn't actually talked *to* him, I realized now. But I unloaded everything I had, leaving out only Lynda's misadventure in Mac's house. Deliberately, I ended with Molly Crocker's bombshell about Renata and Matheson as a buildup to our own suspicion of Chalmers.

"I was, of course, aware of that most unfortunate dalliance," Mac said.

"Of course,"I snapped, peeved at his attitude. "Then maybe you're also aware that your own house guest is the killer."

"House guest?" If Mac had one of his big cigars in his mouth right then it would have fallen out.

"Woollcott Chalmers," Lynda said with deliberation, twisting the knife.

"Ah, Jefferson, Lynda—" He looked from one to the other of us with sadness.

"Did somebody take my name in vain?"

All three of us looked around.

Chalmers, his face screwed into a smile, was holding tight to Renata like a metaphor of dependency.

Lynda pulled the *Beeton's Christmas Annual* out of the brown bag we'd swiped from the underwear drawer in Chalmers's room. She thrust it in front of the old man's face. "Is this what it seems to be?"

Chalmers took it from her and sank down into a chair to page through the annual with painstaking care. "Yes," he said finally, "it is absolutely authentic. This is wonderful! Where did you get it?"

"From your dresser in the McCabes' guest suite," Lynda said.

Mac pulled on his beard and Renata gasped.

"You went into my dresser? This is an outrage!" Chalmers sputtered.

"At least a lapse of etiquette," I agreed. "But not as impolite as murder."

Chalmers beseeched Mac. "Perhaps you can tell me what your brother-in-law is ranting about."

Mac ignited a cigar. Apparently this was no time to obey the NO SMOKING signs, which he usually did in less stressful situations. (Friday night when he used the lit cigar to break the balloon didn't count because that fit into the category of "just showing off.")

"I am afraid, Woollcott, that Jefferson believes you killed Hugh," he said between puffs to stoke up. "If I perceive the scenario correctly, your motives were primarily jealousy and secondarily to retrieve the stolen Sherlockiana which was in Hugh's possession."

"But I didn't have the *Beeton's*," the old man protested. "Somebody must have put it in that drawer. You tell them, Renata."

She seemed somehow to pull away from her husband, distancing herself from him, without physically moving at all. "I don't go into your drawers, Woollcott. You wouldn't like that."

Chalmers grew older, smaller, in his chair.

"We didn't think jealousy was the main motive at all," Lynda said. "It was the blow to his pride when he found out that he was being cuckolded, the realization that Matheson had taken away from him something that he regarded as his."

Renata stepped away from her husband, a look of horror mixed with fear on her face. At least, that's how I read it. I could have sworn she believed he'd killed her lover.

Summoning up a reserve of strength, Chalmers tightened his grip on the arms of his chair and peered up at us with a fierce look. "How dare you people pry into my personal affairs? You have no damned right to invade my privacy with your amateur meddling!" He reminded me of the villain in a Sherlock Holmes story I read once, the one with the snake.

"Woollcott," Mac said with a surprising gentleness, "the matter is scarcely a secret within the Anglo-Indian Club."

Chalmers slumped back into the chair, as if exhausted. "Renata is a young woman and I am an old man." His voice was distant and dry, like the sound of old newspapers rustling together. "I couldn't blame her for having a little fling with Matheson. I knew it was merely physical."

"I'm not . . . I'm not . . . a *tramp*," his wife said, gripping the back of Chalmers's chair. In the weird, surreal circumstances it struck me as an old-fashioned word. She closed her eyes and breathed deeply for a second. "My needs were not just physical. I could never make you understand that, Woollcott. I loved you and I wanted your companionship—I wanted to talk to you about art and music and films. But you were so absorbed in that collection . . . Hugh at least pretended to be interested in me. I was fool. I knew his reputation, but somehow I convinced myself it was different with me, that we had something real."

Chalmers stared straight ahead as he talked about his wife as though she weren't there. "I had no reason to kill Matheson. I knew if I forced Renata to choose between him and me our marriage would be over, so I decided to endure it as long as they were discreet. I was sure that Matheson would soon tire of her and move on to some new conquest, although that hadn't happened yet."

"Discreet?" I echoed. "Molly Crocker heard you and Matheson arguing about it in a bar before a meeting of the Anglo-Indian Club!"

"That was an aberration, something that only happened once. He'd just lost an important case that day and had too much to drink. Apparently he felt the need to mortify me by a graphic explication of his relationship with my wife. That's how I first found out about it."

"And you couldn't stand the public humiliation," I said. "That's why you killed Matheson."

"I assure you, Renata knows quite well that I did not."

She looked away from him.

"That book from your dresser drawer says otherwise," Lynda told Chalmers. "That's why you bopped me on the head to keep me from finding it."

In response to shocked looks all around, we gave the *Cliffs Notes* version of Lynda's morning adventure.

"Why would Woollcott render Lynda unconscious to prevent her from finding the *Beeton's*, then leave it in the drawer?" Mac objected. "That is, even assuming he had the physical stamina to do so."

"He was scared away by the sound of me calling for Lynda," I reasoned. "Things aren't always so neat in real life."

"Granted, but you're saying our killer was so frightened by your arrival that he forgot the object of his quest?" Mac said. "That is hardly likely. And getting past you once you were in the house would have been impossible. There is no exit directly outside from the guest suite. Moreover, from the timetable that you have presented, all of the events at my house must have taken place during my talk on 'Humor in the Canon.'"

"So?" Lynda said.

"So I personally noted Woollcott's presence in the audience during my entire talk. I assure you, he could not possibly have been the individual who hit you over the head, my dear Lynda."

Chapter Thirty-Two
On the Hook

The earth twirled on its axis and revolved around the sun. Eons passed as Woollcott Chalmers stared at Lynda and me, letting Mac's last words hang in the air like humidity in August. Renata looked confused, as if unsure whether to accept the witness that her husband wasn't a murderer after all.

Finally, Lynda said, "Maybe we went around the curves a little too fast with this idea."

"If that's supposed to be an apology," Chalmers said, "I'll have to talk to my lawyer before I accept."

"This game has gone on too long," Mac said. "I must tell you that the murderer is—"

"Mr. Chalmers!"

It wasn't an accusation this time, just the always-annoying Graham Bentley Post calling to Chalmers from the doorway. Even on a Sunday afternoon the man from the Library of Popular Culture was dressed for business. His three-piece gray suit had the requisite stripes and if the shirt had any more starch in it, it would have been one big Roman collar. His thick, gray mustache was trimmed with precision.

"I have interrupted nothing important, I trust." Post's manner as he approached Chalmers was so patently ingratiating that it almost made me ill.

"Nothing important," Chalmers agreed with a sideways glance at Lynda and me.

Post ignored the byplay and heard what he wanted to hear as he approached the old man. "Good, because what I have to say *is* important, Mr. Chalmers. It is about the Woollcott Chalmers Collection."

"Then you should be saying it to these men, not to me." He waved vaguely in the direction of Mac and me. "They represent St. Benignus College, which for good or ill owns the Collection now."

"Not irrevocably," Post said with a triumphant smirk. "It is quite obvious that the collection has been treated shabbily by its new owner. Books have been stolen, a man murdered. The college clearly has not maintained the security of the collection as promised in the agreement under which you made your donation. As a result, I believe that the donation can be voided, freeing you to put the Chalmers Collection in the hands of an institution that is prepared to give it the proper care it deserves."

"Such as the Library of Popular Culture," Lynda interpreted.

Post executed a little bow in her direction. "I am virtually certain our lawyers can make it happen."

"Your lawyers," Mac drawled, "will have to go through me and the college's lawyers first. They will find the task neither easy nor enjoyable."

"On the contrary," Post said. "You don't know my lawyers. These particular legal talents *will* enjoy it. In the case of the Renfield Collection of Disney cartoon cells—"

Lynda pulled on my arm and kept pulling until we were through the doors of the Hearth Room. "I couldn't stand anymore of that," she explained.

"It wasn't a lot of fun," I agreed. "I guess we aren't very good sleuths. We kind of made fools out of ourselves back there."

"What do you mean, 'kind of'? We'll never live this down. McCabe won't let us."

We started wandering through Muckerheide Center. I took Lynda's hand and she didn't jerk it back. I still wasn't sure where our relationship was going, but at least it looked like we had one. So I wasn't as depressed as I should have been about the fiasco we were leaving behind us.

"Maybe Post killed Matheson," I said. "He was on Mac's list. And look at how he benefits from this whole mess if he can use it to convince Chalmers to back legal action against the college."

Lynda shook her head. "That's too indirect and too uncertain to be a motive for murder."

"I know," I sighed as we passed the President's Dining Room, "but it's too bad. I'd love seeing that prig in prison gray."

"What do you suppose Mac has up his sleeve?"

"Don't ask me. As far as he's concerned I'm just his idiot Watson. He hasn't even explained to me the part about Matheson not stealing the books. That could be the solution to the murder for all I know."

Without destination in mind we found ourselves heading aimlessly down the back stairs. The main level of Muckerheide looked as if it had been hit by a neutron bomb. The bookstore, the gallery, the main dining room were all dark. The only living being in sight was the Viking girl at the information desk and the only sound was the small TV she was watching, probably WWE wrestling.

As we kept walking down the stairs toward the next level, Lynda pulled the agenda for the colloquium out of her purse.

"This is practically a timetable of events leading up to the murder," she said. "There must be a clue in here somewhere. It always worked for HerculePoirot."

"Max Cutter does not use timetables."

She went on, ignoring me. "Obviously, the crucial time period is between the end of Kate's talk—Matheson was still alive then—and when I found the body an hour or so later. Where was everybody then?"

I mentally worked my way through Mac's list. "I don't know about Pfannenstiel, Pinkwater, or Post—three P's in a pod!—but we're not looking at any of them as serious suspects. Molly Crocker and Noah Queensbury alibi each other. Renata Chalmers was getting dressed and putting her hair up in those fancy ringlets. Her husband supposedly was discussing some obscure point in a Sherlock Holmes story with Mac, but you've effectively questioned that."

By now we were on the lowest level of Muckerheide Center. The game room was still open, attracting a few stranded dormies, but not many.

"And now Mac is giving Chalmers an alibi again," Lynda mused. "Chalmers couldn't have hit me on the head. But wait a minute! It didn't have to be the killer who did that. If you and I figured out that Chalmers had the book, somebody else could have done the same thing—somebody bent on stealing it."

So Mac could be wrong. Or maybe he didn't have to be. My brother-in-law never stopped playing games, especially word games. Had he ever actually said that Chalmers wasn't guilty? I wasn't sure. What I remembered was Mac talking as if the coroner's report and the TV segment on the Chalmers Collection revealed something critical to the case.

"There's something in my office I think we ought to take a look at," I told Lynda. "It might be the answer to the whole thing."

"What whole thing? What are you talking about?"

"A video of the—"

I shut up. We'd just turned a corner and encountered a horrendous sight. Staring malevolently at a row of soft drink and snack machines was Oscar Hummel. The source of his anguish was elementary to someone who knew the chief as well as I did: He had just worked himself up to having to actually *buy* cigarettes, then had gone looking for a cigarette vending machine, only to realize that there isn't a single such mechanism on campus.

Oscar heard our footsteps and whirled around.

"Teal!" He managed a smile, of a sort. "You're a lifesaver. I need—"

"The love of a good woman," Lynda told him. "But what you want is a cigarette. Sorry, Chief, I quit. Remember? Let me buy you a root beer."

With a grunt and a sour expression on his face, Oscar ungraciously accepted the offer. Lynda bought Diet Cokes for the two of us and a Dad's Root Beer for Oscar. Drinks in hand, we took over a little Formica-topped table in a grimy alcove. I wanted to get out of there, to take Lynda to my office and show her something, but there was no way to exit gracefully. Besides, I wanted to hear what the official investigation had turned up.

"You saved me some shoe leather," Oscar said. "I was just about to go looking for you guys."

"So, Chief," I said, putting it on the professional level, "did you find the gun?"

Oscar knocked back his Dad's as if it were his favorite brew, a local product called Hudepohl 14K. "No gun. And our second witness says Kane wasn't the redhead she saw coming out of Matheson's room." The expression on his face was disappointment and a little more, maybe discomfort. "A redheaded man *and* a blondish woman, it turns out. That's what the witness saw. Funny coincidence, that's just what I'm seeing now as I look at you two."

"Funny," Lynda agreed, looking grim. "But actually I've never thought of myself as exactly a blonde. I'd say my hair leans more toward light brown."

"I consider it dark honey," I chipped in. My stomach felt like some sailor had been using it for knot-tying practice.

Oscar drummed his right hand on the table, like he didn't know what to do without a cigarette in it. "I don't like coincidences. So I asked a few questions, Teal, and I found out that you spent a lot of time hanging around Matheson yesterday."

She shrugged. "I already told you I sat next to him a few times. We talked about Sherlock Holmes."

"And that's all—with Matheson's reputation as a lady-killer and your thing with Jeff here on the rocks?" He shook his head. "That's hard to believe. No, I figure you got a lot cozier than that. He probably gave you the key card to his room. It wasn't on his body or anywhere in the room. Then Jeff walked in on you two later. Anybody who knows Jeff knows how jealous he is when it comes to you. Goodbye lawyer."

"What!" I could feel myself starting to sweat.

"When we were talking earlier today it was obvious you were trying to point the finger at somebody, almost anybody—Molly Crocker, Al Kane. Now I can see you were really just pointing away from you."

This was my worst nightmare come true. "You can't be serious, Oscar."

"Am I laughing? Believe me, old buddy, I take no pleasure in this. In fact, it's hurting me more than it is you."

Before I could express my sincere doubt about that, Lynda said, "Bullshit. You're eating this up. But your stupid theory makes no sense. Why would I leave the room with Jeff if he'd killed a man I'd been intimate with, which by the way I hadn't? Why would I be telling you right now that you're crazy instead of putting the finger on him?"

"I don't know. Maybe it's because you like the idea that a man killed for you."

Lynda threw up her hands with an appropriate amount of drama. "I give up. Oscar, you are certifiable."

Oscar took a long pull on his root beer. "We'll see what my witness says when she sees you two. Meanwhile, why don't you just empty your purse for me?"

"What for?" Lynda said.

"To see if you have Matheson's missing room key."

"Are you trying to humiliate me just because you can't bum cigarettes off of me anymore?"

Oh, damn. She did still have the key. No, she couldn't have been that stupid. But so much had happened,maybe she'd had no time to think about it . . . The knots in my stomach grew tighter.

"So you won't let me look in your purse?" Oscar said.

"I'd feel violated."

"Uh-huh." He ostentatiously twiddled his thumbs.

"You don't have a search warrant," I pointed out.

Oscar raised his eyebrows, all innocence. "You know, I was really hoping I was wrong and we wouldn't have to go the search warrant route, the line-up—"

"Okay, okay," Lynda said. "I'll open my damned purse."

She pulled the gray-blue leather bag off of her lap by its strap and raked the contents out on the Formica table top, carefully avoiding the water rings from our drinks.

The variety was incredible: a change purse, a wad of crumpled tissues, three packs of gum (all opened), a key chain with a little canister of mace, a wallet, Lynda's Android, one loose key, a plastic tampon holder, a rosary, assorted loose change, four pieces of hard candy (Werther's), a notebook, a pen, a pencil, six bobby pins, a nail clipper, two tickets stubs from a 2008 Cincinnati Reds game, a compact, the agenda for "Investigating Arthur Conan Doyle and Sherlock Holmes," a sucker, a checkbook, a hair brush, and a Sussex County map.

Oscar picked up the key chain and squinted at each key in turn. There must have been a dozen of them.

"You're enjoying this, aren't you?" I griped.

"Not me," Oscar said, but I didn't believe him. He had reasons to have it in for Lynda, and he wasn't a particularly forgiving kind. "I don't know why you have all these keys, but none of 'em's from the Winfield."

"I know," Lynda said. I knew, too, because none of them was a key card.

Oscar held up the one loose key and I saw that it was the key to Mac's house. He studied it, shook his head, and gave that, too, back to Lynda. She passed it on to me in a casual, unobtrusive gesture beneath the table that Oscar wasn't supposed to catch but did. He snickered. I knew what he was thinking and I didn't bother to set him straight.

"Now empty out the change purse," he ordered.

Lynda looked at me, sighed, and complied.

This is it, I thought. I made up my mind that if I had to toss up the contents of my wrenching stomach I'd do it in Oscar's substantial lap.

But there was no key card amid the quarters, dimes, nickels, pennies, and blessed medals in the change purse.

Lynda started to put things back in the purse.

"The wallet!" Oscar cried out.

He reached across the table and jerked it out of Lynda's hand. I knew that wallet: It was a Coach, a present from me on Lynda's twenty-sixth birthday, a little more than three years ago. We'd been dating less than a year at the time. Slowly, at Oscar's demand, Lynda unfolded all the little flaps and windows where one might stick a key card.

Might, but hadn't. The Winfield key wasn't in there among the paper money and the plastic credit cards, either.

Oscar slammed the wallet on the table in front of Lynda and stood up, letting his chair clatter to the floor behind him. "You win this round," he barked, "but that doesn't mean I'm through with you two."

Chapter Thirty-Three
The Adventure of the Empty House

Even with Oscar long gone from the game room, I lowered my voice before I asked Lynda, "Where's the key?"

"In the mail," she said, scooping everything back into her purse. "I sent it back to the hotel this morning when I realized how incriminating it could be."

"Very clever. You're not only smart, which I always knew, you have the makings of a great criminal. I just wish you'd told me that before. The information would have added years to my life."

"Sorry. We were always talking about other things. How long do you think it'll take for Oscar to realize he should still parade us before his star witness?"

I gulped the last of my caffeine-free Diet Coke, barely thinking about what the acid in soda can do to a nail. "Only as long as it takes him to stop being so peeved that it clouds his judgment. But maybe after we look at the DVD in my office it won't matter."

We walked across the campus, hand in hand once more, and we fell to talking about the Chalmerses' marital mess.

"I believe in marriage and I believe in forever," Lynda said. "And when I get married I want to make sure it *is* forever. For that, love is essential but not sufficient. It's not nearly enough. I saw that close up. I think my parents loved each other in their own way, but that didn't keep them married. I don't want to screw up the way they did."

This was not new conversational territory for us, but the circumstances were somewhat different than in the past given that—so far as I knew—we were no longer dating. We were, however, holding hands. What was she trying to tell me by bringing this up? More importantly, what was I supposed to say?

One thing for sure, this conversation was not about Lynda's parents, who had met in the Army and had divorced years ago. I didn't know much about them, not even their names, because the subject didn't come up much, except in negative contexts like this one. Theirs was not a close family.

With the wisdom of age, I decided that the safest course was to ask a question and not venture any opinions.

"Well, then, theoretically," I said, backing slowly into a delicate subject, "other than love, what would you be looking for in a husband?"

"A partner," she said without hesitation. *That word again!* "And you can't have a partnership without two strong parties. So I'd have to be able to hold up my end of the deal. I mean, I'd want to be far enough along in my own life and career to have a strong sense of my personal identity."

"Whew," I said, "I'm glad to hear you're not planning on marrying for money. That means I'm still in the running."

"Don't get ahead of yourself."

We shared a nervous laugh as we entered my little office on the first floor of Carey Hall, but I filed the conversation away for future reflection.

My office is crammed with books and binders, file cabinets, campus publications, newspapers, and a television with a DVD player/recorder. Every day I record the Cincinnati news programs in case they have an item on St. Benignus. Most of the stories show up on their websites, of course, but if they slander us I don't want to count on that.

"Now are you going to tell me what this is all about?" Lynda asked as I fast-forwarded through the TV4 Action News weather and the opening segment of Mandy Petrowski's report about the thefts and the colloquium.

"I don't think I'll have to tell you. Just watch."

I pushed the remote to slow down the action just after the exterior shots of me talking outside the library gave way to video of Woollcott Chalmers pointing with his cane to a bust of Sherlock Holmes.

"Moran had planned to shoot the detective at night from across the street, using an air gun specially manufactured by the blind mechanic Von Herder," Chalmers was saying.

I punched the stop-action button, freezing the old collector's image on the screen. "That's it," I said.

Lynda shook her head. "Sorry. Maybe my brain is out of whack from that knock on the head, but I don't get it. What did he say that's so important?"

"Just two words: Air gun. Look, Chalmers has a real bust of Sherlock Holmes in his collection, why not a real air gun to go with it? That's the real reason why the coroner's report said there was no powder burns or 'tattooing' on the victim's body, and also why nobody heard the shots. No wonder Mac found this TV report 'highly suggestive' about the weapon."

She looked skeptical. "Do air guns shoot .32 bullets?"

"You know I don't know anything about guns, except what I research for my mystery writing. But even if they don't, Chalmers could have had it specially built— that's what Chalmers said Colonel Sebastian Moran did in 'The Adventure of the Empty House.'"

"That's a little far-fetched, isn't it?"

"Not with the kind of people we're dealing with here, Lynda—people who have little drawings of Sherlock Holmes on their checks and 221B on their license plates.

And Chalmers put a Stradivarius in his Holmes collection—
a violin worth as much as the stolen books or more, for
crap's sake. The man has the money to feed his obsession."

"But we didn't find anything like an air gun in Mac's
guest suite," Lynda protested.

"We weren't looking for it." I turned off the DVD
player/recorder and the TV. "And as soon as we found the
Beeton's Christmas Annual we stopped searching. It'll be
different this time."

Lynda touched my arm as we neared the door to the
suite at Mac's house. "I still don't like this."

"I guess not," I said, "considering what happened
the last time you were here. How's your head?"

"Huge. Let's get this over with."

We started with the sitting room, figuring that
Lynda had had little time to explore it earlier before she'd
been lured away by a noise. It was a small, sparsely
furnished room which, like the bedroom, featured a picture
window with a glorious view of the Ohio River below us.
The window was framed by bookcases full of old detective
novels. We moved the bookcases and checked behind them,
but no dice. A closet-cum-dressing area ran the length of
the wall opposite, and we gave that close attention with the
same result. The love seat was rattan, so there was no place
to hide anything under it. Feeling the pillows revealed no
suspicious lumps.

"Bedroom next," I said with more hope than faith.

We spent five minutes revisiting the familiar
territory of the dressers and bed. I was standing on a
captain's chair peering into the box at the top of the red and
black curtains when Lynda called, "Over here."

She stood between the bed and a clothes tree draped
with what I took to be Chalmers's jacket, a deerstalker cap
and a pair of Renata's slacks. I focused on the cap, partially
hidden by the jacket so that neither of us had noticed it

earlier. But that wasn't what Lynda wanted me to see. She held up Chalmers's cane.

"It was leaning there, in the umbrella stand at the bottom of the clothes tree where you could hardly see it," she said. "Why would Chalmers leave it behind and go limping around the way he has since yesterday evening?"

I got down from the captain's chair and took the cane to look it over. "This damned thing is heavier than my car. I bet it's what he brained you with."

It looked like solid wood, except for an inch-wide band of silver running around the neck just below the handle. The band was inscribed: "To James Mortimer, M.R.C.S., from his friends of the C.H.H. 1884." The words were out of Sherlock Holmes, I was pretty sure. So I ignored them and looked over the length of the cane for evidence that it had been hollowed out and filled with lead or something equally suitable for skull-bashing.

"Take the tip off," Lynda suggested, pointing to a bit of dirty beige rubber at the bottom of the cane. When I did, I found myself looking down the barrel of something wicked.

"We can quit looking for the air gun," I said. "This answers your question of why Chalmers quit carrying the cane: Some of his Sherlockian friends must know about this little beauty. He was afraid that, seeing him with it, they'd put two and two together."

Lynda might have said something then but for the horrible sound that erupted, like a volcano, coming down Half Moon Street. It was Mac's Chevy. The awful racket reached a peak and then cut out altogether as Mac killed the engine in his driveway. I held on to the cane with one hand and Lynda with the other and we went to the front of the house.

Kate came through the front door first and immediately saw us in the hallway. But her face had barely registered surprise before her husband and the Chalmerses appeared behind her.

"Well, well," Mac said mildly, waving an unlit cigar. "What's this, a welcoming committee in my own home?"

Chalmers, holding Renata's arm for support, focused his clear blue eyes on the cane in my hand. "What are you doing with that?" he snapped.

"Holding it for the police," I said. "They're generally interested in murder weapons."

Renata sucked in her breath.

"Jeff!" my sister exclaimed.

Chalmers looked appropriately murderous. "This is intolerable! Outrageous! And possibly actionable! Didn't you learn anything from your earlier embarrassment, young man? Maybe I *should* withdraw my gift to your college."

Only Mac remained unruffled through all this. My brother-in-law's face, as much as I could see through the beard, showed only a weary sadness.

"Just in case there's anybody here who doesn't know it," Lynda said, "let me point out that there's an air gun concealed in that cane, and I'm pretty sure Mr. Chalmers used it to kill Hugh Matheson."

Mac sighed. "He most certainly did not. Tell them, Renata."

She shook her head. "I can't. I'm sorry, but I can't. If you want me to be the loyal wife, to say that Woollcott couldn't have committed the murder, I can't do that."

"What I want," Mac said, "is for you to tell the truth. That you yourself killed Hugh."

Chapter Thirty-Four
End of the Game

In the deep silence that followed, Renata looked around as if trying to read our faces. The hallway grew smaller.

"You can't be serious," she told Mac in a choked voice.

"How fervently I wish that I were not!" Mac said. "We had better sit down, all of us. This will not come easy or quick."

Chalmers and Renata exchanged looks that nobody but them would understand, then followed Kate into the McCabes' long living room. Lynda and I came next, with Mac hanging back as if uneager.

Once in the room, my brother-in-law enthroned himself in his favorite fireside chair. Kate flanked him on the other side of the bar in a matching wingback, while Lynda and I sat in two other chairs and the Chalmerses shared the couch.

"It was all perfectly obvious from the first," Mac said, looking longingly at his cigar. "Obvious, that is, that Woollcott was supposed to be guilty of killing Hugh. He apparently had not just one motive for revenge but two— books and Renata. You all know the sordid details of the latter, as did I and several others.

"What I did not know, but soon began to suspect, was that Woollcott's cane is actually a specially machined air gun, probably powered by a CO_2 cartridge."

Mac motioned with the cigar at the cane/gun, which I held loosely between the legs in front of me.

"It was designed, of course, to emulate the one made for Colonel Sebastian Moran," Mac said. "Cane guns were quite popular in those days. We know from 'The Adventure of the Empty House' that Moran's air gun fired soft revolver bullets, although the caliber was unspecified. Woollcott's weapon here fires standard .32 bullets, not the customary air rifle pellets. It was very custom-made indeed."

"Not a very powerful weapon, however," Chalmers said. "Or so I was warned."

"That's why the bullet didn't go all the way through, not because it was fired from a distance," Mac said. "The gun was fired at close range into Hugh Matheson's carotid artery. High power wasn't needed. Of far more importance was that the gun was virtually silent, which is helpful if you plan to shoot someone in a hotel room."

I let go of the cane for a moment and rubbed my sweating hands on my pants leg.

"Yet another strong indication that Woollcott had murdered Hugh was the missing *Beeton's Christmas Annual* which Lynda and Jefferson found in his room here. Obviously, Woollcott retrieved the book after killing the one who had stolen it from Muckerheide Center.

"Unfortunately"—Mac allowed himself an ironic smile—"I have a penchant for rejecting the obvious. Perhaps that reflects too many years of writing mystery stories and even more years of reading them, but it has served me well. Woollcott was altogether too convenient a killer. Additionally, I knew that he had been in my sight virtually from the moment we left this house last night until Jefferson and Lynda entered the President's Dining Room. And I knew that he had been in the audience all through my talk this morning when Lynda was struck. Jefferson and Lynda were free to suspect that I was mistaken on both counts, but I knew that I was not."

Lynda paused in the middle of unwrapping a stick of gum. "We figured it didn't have to be the killer who hit me. It could have been another Sherlockian who wanted the *Beeton's*."

"And left without it?" Mac's voice was rich with skepticism. "A thief who failed to find the book himself would have waited for Lynda to find it before he knocked her out. No, the killer assaulted Lynda and the killer left that book behind because the killer wanted it found. Why? To frame Woollcott Chalmers. And who could comfortably enter this house and do that? Eliminating myself and those in this room with no conceivable motive, I was left with an unpleasant but inescapable confirmation of a conclusion I had already reached: Renata Chalmers was that killer."

Renata flinched. She was sitting up straight on the couch, about a foot from her husband. The old man stared at her, but she gave Mac her full attention. "Go on," she said. "Play your game."

"Hugh's mysterious visitor in the deerstalker must have been someone he knew, for he chose to open the door," Mac said. "Renata certainly qualifies on that score. And the cap—Woollcott's, of course—would make a good disguise for a woman with long hair, à la Irene Adler dressing as a man in 'A Scandal in Bohemia.' You will recall that Renata was already wearing a suit with slacks yesterday."

"Hold it, Mac," Lynda interrupted. "You mentioned long hair. Renata may not have been with her husband at the time of the murder, but we know she was putting her hair into ringlets to go with her Victorian outfit for the evening. I saw her earlier in the day and I saw her later with her hair fixed up and I know from experience how long that work can take."

Renata flashed her a look of gratitude. But Kate said, "Not if you just put on a wig with the ringlets already on it."

My sister sat forward in her chair. "Mac, is that why you asked me this morning whether Renata's hair—"

"Exactly. Now Jefferson, think back to your first visit to the guest suite this morning. Undoubtedly you looked around at the dressers before Renata stopped you. Did you see a curling iron? No? I thought not. How about a wig?"

I closed my eyes and tried to bring it all back. Yes, in my mental image there was a lump of hair sitting with the jewelry box and the makeup and the hair brush. But was it just the power of Mac's suggestion that had put it there? Unsure, I shook my head. "Sorry, Mac, I can't—"

"Yes," Woollcott Chalmers said, looking at his wife. "Renata brought one of her hairpieces. I never thought . . ." He licked his lips and fell silent.

"But there wasn't any hair when Jeff and I searched the room for the book," Lynda said.

"Of course not," Mac agreed. "Renata removed it after she knocked you unconscious. Perhaps she secreted it in that large handbag she carries. The question would be easily settled, Renata, if you would care to let us look inside."

"No!" For a second her eyes were wild, like a cornered animal. "That suggestion is insulting."

"I did not think you would like it." Again Mac turned his attention to Lynda and me. "Renata undoubtedly knew that her flimsy alibi would fall apart if you realized that her elaborate Victorian coiffure was the work of a few moments. Hence her need to knock you out, Lynda, and spirit away the wig. However, her primary reason for being in the suite was to plant the *Beeton's* in her husband's drawer so that it would be there to incriminate him when you two looked for it."

"This is all speculation," Renata said in a firm voice. "You have no proof for any of it."

"Perhaps not," Mac conceded. "What would happen, however, if the police showed your photograph around the Winfield? Is there no one who would remember such a strikingly attractive woman in the hotel around the time of the murder? I suspect you kept the deerstalker in your handbag, not on your head, until you reached the proper floor. And then there is the matter of that cane, which I am quite certain will turn out to be the murder weapon. It was used to throw suspicion on Woollcott, but you had equal access to it, Renata. And Woollcott has an alibi for the murder, which you lack."

The fight went out of Renata. She stared at the dried flower arrangement in front of the fireplace screen.

"Why?" her husband breathed. "Why, Renata?"

"And how come you had to come back when I was here?" Lynda asked. Unconsciously her right hand stole to the tender part at the back of her head. She winced.

Renata looked at her with a strangely graceful, almost regal movement in which she moved her head but not her body. "I am sorry about that, Lynda. I had intended to slip the book into Woollcott's dresser this morning, after he and our hosts left for the symposium. But then your friend showed up." Renata nodded at me. "I thought he was there to search for the book—and I was certain that he'd be back."

"Nothing could have been better for your plans, of course," Mac said.

"Of course," Renata agreed. "It meant I wouldn't have to somehow maneuver Kate into 'discovering' the book as I had planned. The trick was to plant the book in an easily uncovered hiding place before Jeff returned. When I saw him leave the lecture hall with Bob Nakamora, that was my opening. With him out of the way, I didn't expect any company here. When you showed up, Lynda, thatcompletely unnerved me. That's why I hit you—not because I was afraid you'd see the wig. Taking the wig was an afterthought. I grabbed it and ran. I must have been running through the kitchen and out the back of the house about the time Jeff was coming in the front."

"And from there we played right into your hands," I said with a bitterness I could almost taste.

"Not entirely." She was a cool one, seemingly unfazed by the collapse of her carefully contrived plans. "You were supposed to find the gun right away. I hid it from Woollcott yesterday when we came back to change our clothes because I knew I was going to use it on Hugh. And I kept it hidden today until Woollcott was out of the house."

"Wait a minute," I said. "What did you think happened to it, Chalmers? I'm sure you don't just misplace unique objects like that."

"Actually, he does," Renata said coldly before he could answer. "His memory is failing along with several functions, except when it comes to his damned Sherlock Holmes. After he was out of the house, I put it where you should have seen it the first time."

"Sorry to disappoint you," Lynda murmured.

"But why?" Kate cried. "Why frame your husband? Why kill your lover?"

"Lover?" Renata repeated, unconsciously forming a fist with her right hand. Her icy coolness was slipping. "He didn't love me. Neither of them did. I was a possession, a trinket, another collectible for the two of them to squabble over. That's just what I heard them doing in the bar one night before an Anglo-Indian Club meeting. I decided that this was one battle of male egos they would both lose. I would make them pay. It was only a matter of waiting for the right moment. The moment came and I did it and I'm glad I did it and the only thing I'm sorry about is that Woollcott didn't suffer enough."

She sat back, exhausted, but without loosening her posture.

"I am reminded," said Mac, "of a Persian proverb quoted by Sherlock Holmes in 'A Case of Identity'—'There is danger for him who taketh the tiger cub, and danger also for whoso snatches a delusion from a woman.'"

Chalmers blinked and fidgeted with his hands, a man who knew something awful had happened to him but didn't understand quite what. Lynda turned to him.

"You must have known," she said. "You must have realized Renata killed your old rival, and yet you kept silent."

"How could I have guessed?" His old eyes darted around the room, pathetic and pleading.

"You knew your air gun was missing and you knew your wife didn't really have an alibi," Lynda said. "You're too shrewd not to have added it all up."

"We never spoke of it," he said. I leaned forward to hear. "But I did suspect. I thought she did it for me—because Matheson stole my books, stole my whole life practically."

Renata stood up, arms folded, and laughed in a way that sent bumps goose-stepping down my spine. "I stole your precious books, you silly old fool, not Hugh. That was part of the setup, to give you a solid motive for killing him. I knew that jealousy over *me* wasn't enough."

She paced in front of the fireplace, no more than a couple of feet in front of me, suddenly overcome with nervous energy.

"It was clear to me early on that you took those books," Mac said. "'When you have eliminated the impossible, whatever remains, however improbable, must be the truth.' There was no forced entrance into the exhibit room. The keys were all accounted for and there were no obvious indications that a duplicate had been made. Ergo, *there was no burglary.* On Friday afternoon, when you and Woollcott visited the display, you grabbed those three books when you were unobserved and took them away in that immense handbag of yours, didn't you?"

Mac seemed to take Renata's stony silence for assent. "I was certain that you didn't do it out of a simple desire to possess the books. Why, then? I concluded it was an attempt to malign Hugh, the most likely suspect in the theft based on motive. I didn't know why, however. Hugh didn't appear to be in any imminent danger of arrest, so I kept my thoughts to myself until I could see what you were up to. Possibly that decision of mine cost a man his life, and I shall have to live with that guilty knowledge for the rest of mine. When Hugh was killed, Renata, I suspected you at once."

I whirled on my brother-in-law, barely holding myself together as my voice rose. "You knew it was her and you let me run around acting like an amateur detective in a stupid book, making a fool out of myself for nothing?" This was just too much to take without protest.

"By no means was it for nothing, Jefferson! *Au contraire*, your activities were crucial. I needed to know whether any other explanation was possible. I was hoping with all my heart—"

He was still talking when I caught the movement out of the corner of my eye: Renata coming at me. Before I could react she had snatched the cane/gun from my loose grip.

She held the stick in her left hand, the handle in her right, jamming the wicked device up against her husband's ear. Immobilized by panic, Chalmers's eyes widened and his skin turned a color I'd most recently seen on the corpse of Hugh Matheson.

It was all I could do to keep from losing control of my bladder, but Mac barely raised an eyebrow. "Framing your husband was never the end game of the plan, was it, Renata?" he said. "That wouldn't have been enough."

She shook her head. "The evidence was all circumstantial. There was no guarantee he'd be convicted, but I didn't need that. I just needed for him to be suspected as a killer while I was his brave and innocent trophy wife. Then some day when I had to shoot him in self-defense I'd be seen as the real victim, not him. But he is going to be the victim—right now."

With that Renata shoved forward the metallic ring near the top of the cane and turned the decorative handle a quarter-turn to the right. My entire body was tensed for the whoosh of deadly air, the site of blood.

But the sound was muted and nothing happened to Chalmers. Renata's face contorted in shock and fury and she repeated the action. *Click, click, click.* Nothing happened.

Desperate, she turned, first to me and then to Mac. "What have you done?"

From the side pocket of his tweed suit coat, Mac held up a bullet. "It seemed to me that removing the bullet was the prudent thing to do, once I had it figured out. I was a trifle late getting back to the colloquium."

With an inarticulate cry Renata lifted the cane above her head, turning it into a club. Woollcott Chalmers cringed in front of her, still paralyzed with shock. I started to move, but Lynda moved faster.

"Oh, no, you don't," she said, wresting the heavy stick from Renata's hands. "You're not going to hit anybody else with that damned thing."

Chapter Thirty-Five
The Wrap-up

This time I didn't disguise my voice when I called 911. No more Minnie Mouse. Officer Gibbons and a phalanx of Erin's Finest were there on the double, Oscar not among them. I suspect he was chowing down with his mother at the Bob Evans restaurant just off the highway.

That was a few months ago but seems longer as I write this account in mid-summer. In the light of Renata's confession, I'm happy to report that the identities of the man and woman seen outside Matheson's hotel room and that of the person who phoned in the murder have fallen off the chief's radar screen. Or maybe he'd rather not know.

Ralph Pendergast, less forgiving or forgetting, is still spitting nails about the whole business, but there's not much he can do about it. It's kind of hard for him to distance himself from the Chalmers Collection, and thereby all the chaos it wrought, considering that I still have my iPhone video of him speaking so eloquently about St. Benignus being honored to receive the Collection. I haven't posted it to YouTube, but the unspoken threat is there.

Renata Chalmers is still awaiting trial, out on a huge bail posted by her husband. He also hired Aristotle O'Doul, the most prominent criminal defense attorney in the country. Speculation has it that O'Doul is going to try to mount a novel defense based on battered lover syndrome. I wish I had the popcorn concession for that circus.

Lynda's first-person account of the showdown on Half Moon Street won kudos all around, and there are probably some journalism awards awaiting her and maybe a promotion if there is any justice in the world.

You may be wondering about Lynda and me. So am I. I'm not sure that we're dating again, but we're definitely no longer *not* dating. She's changed her Relationship status on Facebook to "It's Complicated," and so have I. Standing over a dead body, concealing information from the police, being accused of murder, facing down a killer—those are bonding experiences when a man and woman do them together. So we're moving toward each other again—at glacial speed and sometimes two steps forward and one step back, but moving nonetheless.

Sebastian McCabe, meanwhile, remains insufferable. He did, after all, solve the murder. Now he's more convinced than ever that I'm his Watson. And now that I've written this, I guess I am.

A FEW WORDS OF THANKS

On behalf of my friend Thomas Jefferson Cody, I wish to express my sincere gratitude to the following family members, friends, and experts whose contributions to the preparation of this manuscript for publication were invaluable:
Ann Brauer Andriacco
Michael J. Andriacco
Felicia Carparelli
Alistair Duncan
Paul D. Herbert
Bill Schrand

Special thanks to Jeff Suess for his editing and proofreading on this second edition.

Whatever errors remain are solely the responsibility of the author and his literary agent.

Dan Andriacco
May 2015

About the Author

Dan Andriacco has been reading mysteries since he discovered Sherlock Holmes at the age of nine, and writing them almost as long. The first five books in his popular Sebastian McCabe — Jeff Cody series are *No Police Like Holmes*, *Holmes Sweet Holmes*, *The 1895 Murder*, *The Disappearance of Mr. James Phillimore*, and *Rogues Gallery*. He is also the co-author, with Kieran McMullen, of *The Amateur Executioner*, *The Poisoned Penman*, and *The Egyptian Curse* mysteries solved by Enoch Hale with Sherlock Holmes.

A member of the Tankerville Club, the Illustrious Clients, the Vatican Cameos, and the John H. Watson Society, and an associate member of the Diogenes Club of Washington, D.C., Dan is also the author of *Baker Street Beat: An Eclectic Collection of Sherlockian Scribblings*. Follow his blog at www.danandriacco.com, his tweets at *@DanAndriacco*, and his Facebook Fan Page at: www.facebook.com/DanAndriaccoMysteries.

Dr. Dan and his wife, Ann, have three grown children and five grandchildren. They live in Cincinnati, Ohio, USA, about forty miles downriver from Erin.

Praise for the McCabe—Cody series

"You're in the hands of a master of mystery plotting here.*Rogues Gallery* is a delightful read, hard to put down, and highly recommended. And did I say fun?"
— Hollywood screenwriter Bonnie MacBird

"The villain is hard to discern and the motives involved are even more obscure. All-in-all, this (*The Disappearance of Mr. James Phillimore*) is a fun read in a series that keeps getting better with each new tale."
—Philip K. Jones

"*The* 1895 *Murder*is the most smoothly-plotted and written Cody/McCabe mystery yet. Mr. Andriacco plays fair with the reader, but his clues are deftly hidden, much as Sebastian McCabe hides the secrets to his magic tricks under an entertaining run of palaver."
—*The Well-Read Sherlockian*

"I loved Dan Andriacco's first novel about Sebastian McCabe and Jeff Cody,and I'm delighted to recommend (*Holmes Sweet Holmes*), which has a curiously topical touch."
—Roger Johnson, *Sherlock Holmes Society of London*

"*No Police Like Holmes*is a chocolate bar of a novel—delicious, addictive, and leaves a craving for more."
—*Girl Meets Sherlock*

 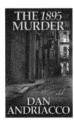 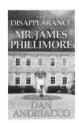 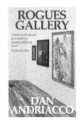

Also from Dan Andriacco and Kieran McMullen

 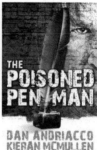 

The Amateur Executioner

The Poisoned Penman

The Egyptian Curse

In contrast to most tales involving Holmes, *The Amateur Executioner* takes us into an ambiguous and murky world where right and wrong aren't always distinguishable. I look forward to reading more about Enoch Hale.

The Sherlock Holmes Society of London

www.mxpublishing.com

Also from MX Publishing

MX Publishing is the world's largest specialist Sherlock Holmes publisher, with over a hundred titles and fifty authors creating the latest in Sherlock Holmes fiction and non-fiction.

From traditional short stories and novels to travel guides and quiz books, MX Publishing cater for all Holmes fans.

The collection includes leading titles such as *Benedict Cumberbatch In Transition* and *The Norwood Author* which won the 2011 Howlett Award (Sherlock Holmes Book of the Year).

MX Publishing also has one of the largest communities of Holmes fans on Facebook with regular contributions from dozens of authors.

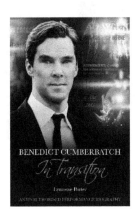

www.mxpublishing.com

Also from MX Publishing

Our bestselling short story collections 'Lost Stories of Sherlock Holmes', 'The Outstanding Mysteries of Sherlock Holmes', 'Untold Adventures of Sherlock Holmes' (and the sequel 'Studies in Legacy') and 'Sherlock Holmes in Pursuit'.

Also from MX Publishing

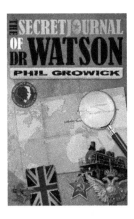

"Phil Growick's, *'The Secret Journal of Dr Watson'*, is an adventure which takes place in the latter part of Holmes and Watson's lives. They are entrusted by HM Government (although not officially) and the King no less to undertake a rescue mission to save the Romanovs, Russia's Royal family from a grisly end at the hand of the Bolsheviks. There is a wealth of detail in the story but not so much as would detract us from the enjoyment of the story. Espionage, counter-espionage, the ace of spies himself, double-agents, double-crossers...all these flit across the pages in a realistic and exciting way. All the characters are extremely well-drawn and Mr Growick, most importantly, does not falter with a very good ear for Holmesian dialogue indeed. Highly recommended. A five-star effort."
The Baker Street Society

The characters return in the sequel
The Revenge of Sherlock Holmes'.

www.mxpublishing.com